Crying Just Like Anybody

Crying Just Like Anybody

The Fiction Desk Anthology Series
Volume Four

Edited by Rob Redman

The Fiction Desk

First published in 2012 by The Fiction Desk Ltd.

ISBN 978-0-9567843-6-0

The Fiction Desk
PO Box 116
Rye
TN31 9DY

Please note that we do not accept postal submissions.
See our website for submissions information.

www.thefictiondesk.com

The Fiction Desk Ltd
Registered in the UK, no 07410083
Registered office: 3rd Floor, 207 Regent Street, London, W1B 3HH

Printed and bound in the UK by Imprint Digital.

Contents

Contents

Introduction

Rob Redman

How personal is publishing?

It's a question that hangs in the background of almost everything I do at The Fiction Desk, from the editorial policy to the cover design.

It's fashionable these days to think of publishing as a technical, financial process in which manuscripts are selected using a spreadsheet and then processed into books with a minimum of human intervention. While we may identify certain imprints with a specific genre or style of writing, it's easy to forget that — large or small — a publisher's list usually represents the individual tastes of an editor, or a small group of editors. And the tastes of those editors in what they choose to publish can be as unique and personal as the books they choose to put on their shelves at home.

Publishers usually foster a semi-anonymous image for themselves: even the terms 'editor' and 'publisher' are confused and vague, especially in smaller publishing operations. The different roles, and who performs them, are rarely defined for the public, and I doubt most readers could name the editors behind even their favourite books. In Italy, the publisher is the *editore* and the editor the *curatore*, which in some ways makes more sense than our own terminology: I'm not talking here about the technical work on the text, which is necessarily invisible and anonymous because the text must always belong to the author, but about the *curatorial* editing.

In the early days of publishing, the publisher's name usually *was* the publisher's name: John Murray, Chapman & Hall, Martin Secker, and so on. When Herbert Jonathan Cape left (Gerald) Duckworth to found his own company in 1919, he may have called it Page & Co at first, but it wasn't long before he rechristened it after himself. These days, new fiction publishers are almost always named for objects, mythological figures, or abstract ideas: Telegram, Hesperus, Peirene, Salt, The Fiction Desk. There are very few recent publishers that use the founder's name for the imprint; offhand, the only one I can think of is Charles Boyle's CB Editions.

There are probably a few reasons for this change in convention, from the phenomenal success of Allen Lane's Penguin brand in the 1930s to the number of imprints now launched by large publishing houses rather than by individuals, and it's by no means a change unique to publishing. Still, I wonder how it has affected readers' perception of publishers, and even publishers' and editors' perception of their own roles.

I have no intention of changing the name of The Fiction Desk, or of introducing a red man as a new logo, but something that's surprised me over the last couple of years has been just how personal my relationship to these books actually is. The stories presented here are very much my own selection; another editor would have chosen different stories from the same set of submissions. (As is normal for a publisher, we often publish stories rejected by other journals, and I've rejected several stories that I've subsequently seen published elsewhere.)

This is carried through to the design of the books: for example, you're reading this in Goudy Old Style because that typeface reflects my own belief in the values of traditional storytelling forms over more experimental techniques.

The introductions to individual stories are also a challenge: how personal should they be? Should they be in my own voice, or in a disembodied generic editorial voice? The former is a more honest and accurate reflection of the curatorial process; the latter perhaps quieter and less distracting from the stories. Should I start popping up from behind the furniture at the start of each story, like Rod Serling at the start of *Twilight Zone* episodes?

No. No, I probably shouldn't. But I'll continue to think about the editor's role, the voice of that role, and where and how that voice should feature in these volumes, aiming to find a balance that renders the curatorial process transparent without detracting from the integrity of the individual stories.

Crying Just Like Anybody

Richard Smyth

He was a little guy: five-two, five-three. His mouth was too wide to fit his face and he didn't have any hair. He sat with his legs neatly crossed on a deal crate and I could see his dirty woollen ankle socks.

I don't know, I said.

Johnny nudged me. *Sure* he is, he said.

I shook my head and said it again: Johnny, I don't know.

The little guy was watching us. He seemed interested.

Sure he is.

I don't know, I said. I mean he doesn't *look* like a Martian.

Sure he does.

Sherrit nek hazzer minny most, the Martian said.

See? said Johnny.

Johnny's Gianni really, but around here no one calls anyone by their right name. There's little Tomas Quis who's Spanish but he's called Tom Keys, and there's my sister Jesca and the boys call her 'Yes' and make dirty jokes about it. At the repair shop Mr White is really Mr Weiss and then there's Si Portman who works for the grocer and wears braces on his legs, and he's just called Dumdum. Johnny ought to be Gianni really but everyone calls him Johnny. He doesn't mind.

He met me after work. I waitress. It was around eleven.

Anna, he said, and grabbed my elbow. Anna's my right name, at least. Anna Möller, with an umlaut. I pulled my elbow away.

*Care*ful, kid, this is a new goddamn *coat*.

It was, too.

You'll never guess, he said.

So you'd better tell me.

Go ahead and guess.

I sighed.

I've been working all day, I said. I'm tired.

Go ahead and guess.

He was all excited about something. He couldn't stop grinning. When he grins you can see where there are two teeth missing in his upper jaw. His father did it one time.

I tried to guess.

Babe Herman went six for six. You found a buck in the street. Clara Bow sent you a postcard.

Nope, Johnny said.

Then I give up.

You won't believe me if I tell you.

What the hell *is* this, Johnny?

Maybe you'd better just see for yourself, Johnny said.

He took hold of my hand. This was all outside the doorway of Henry Moon's place at the ocean end of Depeyster. It wasn't lit and I thought Johnny was going to kiss me there in the dark. I thought it was a hell of a way to lead up to kissing a girl but I was ready to be kissed anyway.

I said: Johnny?

Johnny said something but right then an El train went by overhead and I didn't hear what it was. He didn't kiss me. He just led me by the hand out of the darkness and up Depeyster and on to Front.

Where are we going?

You'll see.

He walked too fast. I had on these high-heeled shoes and I couldn't keep up.

Slow down, dammit. Where's the goddamn emergency?

Johnny just laughed. He led me into an alleyway I didn't even know the name of. *This* is where he kisses me, I thought. And who knows what else. But instead he opened a wormy blue door in the wall and pointed inside. There was a light on. I looked inside and there was this little guy sitting on a deal crate.

He smiled at me.

Who the hell's this? I said.

My father's a teacher. He taught at a school across the bridge until some girl complained. This was in the war. My father's a German. Now he works in the garment district helping the Jews with their taxes and things, but underneath that he's still a teacher. He taught me and my sisters to read and write. I wanted to ask him about Johnny's Martian but I didn't dare. I didn't want to get Johnny into trouble. And I didn't want him to laugh at me.

He was in the kitchen eating livers on toast when I got home. He likes to sit up late. He had a book open and a glass of something.

Good evening, Anna, he said.

My father talks very polite English.

I asked him about Mars. He swallowed the piece of toast he was eating and put a bookmark in his book and closed the book.

Why do you ask?

I shrugged. My father stood up, came round the table, and put his left hand on my shoulder. With his right hand he opened the door to the street.

It was cold out, and my father was only in his shirtsleeves and a singlet underneath, but he didn't seem to mind. We stood side by side on the doorstep. We live on Trundle Row, which is off Catherine Street, which is off Henry Street: we live way out of the way in midtown, is what I mean. There's nothing in Trundle Row but trashcans and cats and fruit crates. Since my mother died no one even sweeps the step.

Beautiful, my father said. Actually he said *wunderschön*, which means the same. He wasn't looking at the trashcans. He was looking up. I looked up too.

Beautiful, I said. I said it in English. It was one of those clear nights and between the gutters of the houses I could see a strip of clear dark sky and maybe a dozen stars.

There, my father said, pointing. Mars.

It just looked like a star.

It has two moons, he said. The moons are called Fear and Panic. We can't see them from here.

I didn't know that, I said. I never knew there was more than one moon.

Out there, my father said, waving a hand at the sky, there are hundreds.

He told me that there are canals on Mars. I asked him who built the canals. Martians, I guess, he said, and laughed. I wondered if the little guy Johnny had found had ever worked on the canals.

He didn't look like he'd be any good at digging or loading coal. But I didn't know what else there was for him to do on Mars.

Phobos and Deimos, my father said.

What?

Greek, he said. Fear and Panic. Phobos and Deimos.

Oh, I said.

It's just like I said. Round here, nobody calls anything by their real names.

Things got out of hand when Joe Gillray got involved. I never wanted him to get involved. The truth is, the whole thing was so crazy, I didn't want to be involved myself, only Johnny never gave me a choice. I wish he hadn't said anything to Joe, though.

We were at Alessandro's. I was drinking a sarsaparilla and Johnny was picking up a dish of cannelloni to take to the Martian. Put a cloth over it, he was saying to Alessandro. Put a cloth over it, for God's sake, or it'll be cold by the time it gets there.

Joe was sitting at a table looking over a newspaper. Knowing Joe I bet he was looking for his own name in the paper. He was an Irishman. Overweight, maybe thirty years old. Was *he* ever a bigshot. He lived with his parents and ran errands for Owney Madden when he wasn't minding the register at his father's tobacconist. He wore a watch chain and a derby hat.

When Johnny said that about the cannelloni getting cold he looked up.

Someone sick?

Why didn't he just say yes? Why couldn't he just say, sure, the old man's laid up with a crick in his back, or the 'flu, or a broken leg, here's his dinner I'm taking him.

No, Johnny said. It's for a guest. A special guest.

Why couldn't he have just kept his damn mouth shut?

Sherrit nek eggy pappy rot es tollit kerrum, said the Martian.

Joe Gillray laughed.

How about that. Get him to say something else.

Johnny prodded the Martian in the ribs.

Leave him be, I said.

He's all right, Johnny said. Aren't you, kid?

He didn't look all right.

Kee ezz azz ember! he said. Nem tudger tanner eyin steyin!

And you just *found* him? Joe Gillray said to Johnny.

He was lying down in the middle of Pearl at three o'clock in the morning, Johnny said. He must've fell from the sky.

Well, well, said Joe Gillray. A man from Mars. Well, well.

Tecky vaggy, said the Martian.

Shut the hell up and eat your goddamn cannelloni, Johnny said.

Well, well, said Joe Gillray.

He could talk; I have to give him that. People say it's 'cause he's Irish but I've known a few Irish boys and all they can say is How about you darlin' and then they put their hand up your skirt. But Joe could talk, all right. I heard him giving his spiel to two Italians on the corner of Depeyster and Front.

You've never seen a thing like it.

Is that a fact?

Sure it's a fact, my friend. Listen, I've been all over. I've seen it all. I've been all around.

Is that a fact?

I don't think the Italians had good English.

Sure it's fact, sure as I'm standing here, I've been all over the world, and when I saw this character, I thought my goddamn heart was going to stop. I thought I was going to drop dead right on the spot!

A spaceman, one of the Italians said.

A real-life man from Mars. Can you even imagine? An emissary, Joe said, from another goddamn galaxy.

A quarter?

That's all I'm asking, Joe said. Each.

I stopped listening after that. I guess Joe got his fifty cents all right.

Then I went to see the Martian. They didn't lock the door or anything, but the Martian stayed there anyway. Where else was he going to go? I went to see him. I talked to him; although I don't know if you can call it talking to somebody when they don't say anything back, and they can't even understand what you're saying in the first place.

So I guess what I did was, I went to see the Martian, and I just talked.

My father says there are canals where you come from, I said.

The Martian was sitting on the floor. Johnny had put down a mattress, blanket, rolled-up sweater for a pillow. The edges of the mattress were dark with damp. I didn't know how the Martian'd been sleeping, or if he'd slept at all. Maybe — what did I know? — he didn't even need to sleep.

He looked tired, though. There was a little grey stubble on his jaw. He nodded and blinked his big lazy eyes.

We got canals here, too, I said. Upstate mostly. I mean, far away. But not far away compared to where you're from. I mean — Schenectady. Syracuse. Out there.

I didn't think he could have been very old. Older than *me*, sure. I'm eighteen, eighteen and two thirds. But if he was just a normal guy I'd have said he was maybe thirty or thirty-five.

Maybe you could get a job there, if you decide you want to stay, I said. On a canal boat. Maybe if you save up the money Johnny and Joe give you, you can buy a ticket and go to Schenectady and work on a canal, or something.

As soon as I said it I felt like... well, I felt all of a sudden like *I* wanted to buy a ticket to Schenectady and take the train and go work on a canal boat. More than I wanted anything. It was only for a second, but it was a crazy feeling. I couldn't work on a canal boat. I waitress, is what I do.

Or maybe you'll be heading home, I said.

The Martian looked up at me and sighed. Then he licked his forefinger, and on the pale concrete floor he drew a '2'.

I wasn't sure what to say. He was looking at me again.

You learned numbers, I said.

Kett, the Martian said.

I wondered how come he had on a blue flannel shirt and pants instead of a flying suit or something. I wondered how he wound up in the middle of Pearl at three o'clock in the morning.

The thing about Johnny was that after he'd tried to put his hand inside your dress a couple of times and been told to cut it out, he wouldn't try it again. I don't say that that was a *good* thing about Johnny. But I guess it made him a damn sight better than a lot of guys, that's all.

Cut it out.

C'*mon*. Joe wants to take him to Coney Island. He thinks we'll —

Cut it *out*, Johnny.

Okay, ok*ay*. He thinks we'll make a fortune there. Show him at Steeplechase Park or whatever they have there. In the freakshow or whatever.

Johnny'd never been to Coney Island. His parents never took him.

We were sitting on the harbourside at the bottom of Coenties Slip. I didn't mind necking and I liked Johnny's arm round my waist but I had on a dress I'd borrowed from my sister — it was cherryblossom pink with a satin rose on one shoulder — and Johnny kept mussing it up. Anyway I wanted to talk about the Martian. I like Johnny but sometimes I want to talk.

It's a shame Barnum's museum burned down, I said. You could have sold him to Barnum for a million bucks.

You think? Johnny said. God *damn*.

He didn't see that I was kidding him.

I asked Johnny if he didn't think he ought to tell the government about the Martian he'd found. Or at least the Mayor's office or somebody.

He said, are you kidding?

I told him no, no I'm not. I was kidding before about Barnum but I'm serious now. People will want to know about this.

Johnny snapped his fingers.

That's it, he said. We'll sell it to the goddamn New York World!

I was sick of talking about it. I took hold of Johnny's hand and put it on my bare knee.

Who put an end to it all in the end was Fat Pete Law. Pete Law was this fat guy who was friends with my father. I think he used to be in city politics or something. Now he was retired and all he did all day was sit around reading books and boozing. My father liked him. My father called him 'the wisest fellow in Manhattan', but I guess he was mostly kidding. With my father it can be hard to tell.

What put an end to it all was I went to see the Martian again. He'd been there three nights. Like I said, where the hell else was he going to go?

When I opened the door he was standing with his back to me and his face to the wall.

Hello, I said, but the Martian didn't turn around. I guess he was pretty tired of being poked by Joe Gillray and gawped at by bums for a quarter a go.

It's just me, I said.

He looked over his shoulder. I thought he'd look sore. I'd have been sore, if I'd been him. But he didn't look sore. First, he looked tired, and because he looked tired he looked old. Second, he looked sad. I never in my life saw a face so sad. He opened his too-wide mouth and gaped like a fish on a slab.

I remember thinking, he's crying, that must be how a man from Mars cries. He made a noise like a seagull: *awk* or *arook*.

Magger emley keztet, he said, engem a lannium. Ozzin yunyero lannio.

And then he was crying just like a man cries, just like anyone cries.

I've tried to repeat all this like he said it, the way he said the things he said, whatever the hell they were, but I know I can't, really, because that was the craziest thing about the Martian. Sure his face was kind of peculiar and he'd been lying in the road at three in the morning, but the way he talked: you listened to him, and it was like Johnny said: you'd believe he was from another planet. It wasn't even like talking. It was like music.

I've been around, Johnny would say, which was true, even though he'd never been to Coney Island. I've been all around this city, and I've heard 'em all, all the lingos, the Bohunks, the Yids, the Swedes, the Krauts, even the Chinese and Japanese; they don't talk this way, nobody talks this way. Nobody on this earth, Johnny would say, talks like the Martian talks. And he was right, I thought.

But here the Martian was, crying just like anybody. He turned away from the wall; he turned to face me.

At first I was scared to touch him — I didn't know if he'd be slimy like a frog or if I might get an electrical shock or something — but then I took hold of his hand, his right hand, and after that I wasn't scared any more. His hand was dry. It was small and the skin was smooth: it didn't feel like the hand of a guy who worked on a canal. I let go of his hand and put my arms around his neck, just because he was crying, just so as he'd stop. The guy had a bad body odour, but I guessed that wasn't his fault.

He breathed out through his mouth and his breath wasn't so great either. That was the garlic from all the goddamn cannelloni Johnny had been feeding him. He put his arms around my waist.

Sherrit nek hazzer minny most, he said, or sang, or whatever.

The sad little Martian kissed my hair and Johnny walked in through the door.

I tried to comb my hair to cover my eye but my dumb hair wasn't long enough. It wasn't like it was the first time I'd been hit, but it was the first time Johnny'd hit me.

Anna?

I have to use the bathroom, Dad, I said.

We had a little bathroom with a pan and a basin that we shared with the Podolskis next door. I didn't know what I was going to do in there anyway, except be by myself for a little while. But my father said: no. Anna, look at me.

So I looked at him.

That's a heck of a shiner, said Fat Pete Law.

The two of them were sitting at our kitchen table with a bottle of something clear. This was maybe seven o'clock in the evening.

My father had his shirtsleeves rolled back. Pete Law was wearing an untied bowtie. Pete Law was said to be a sharp dresser.

My father drummed his fingers once on the tabletop and said: *Wer?*

When he was upset sometimes my father forgot to talk English.

I told him. I told him how Johnny had never done anything like it before but how he must have just lost his head, seeing me there. Johnny had swung his arm just as I was turning around and his fist had hit my face, right in my eye socket. I told him how I figured Johnny must have pulled the punch, because it didn't hurt too much. Johnny had called me a fucking Kraut bitch; I didn't tell my father that. I told him that the Martian had attacked Johnny. He wasn't much of a fighter: he'd caught Johnny a good one on the nose, but he didn't hit hard enough, and Johnny'd folded him up with a punch to his guts. I told him how Johnny'd gone away then.

The main thing was, I told him about the Martian, and I told Pete Law, too.

Martian? my father said. Martin?

My father had a brother named Martin.

No, I said. Now I felt like a crazy person. A man from Mars. A Martian.

My father looked at Pete Law. Pete Law looked at me.

A Martian in Manhattan? Pete Law asked with a smile. I suppose he thought it was funny. He had a good sense of humour, although maybe he had *too* good a sense of humour. Not everything's funny. I don't think it is, anyway. I didn't think this was.

Yeah, I said. Johnny found him in the street.

What a piece of luck, Pete Law laughed.

But my father didn't think it was funny either. I guess he was afraid I was crazy. He took hold of my wrist.

Why do you think this man is a Martian, Anna?, he asked me seriously. Did he *tell* you that he is a Martian?

He doesn't tell me anything, I said. He can't. He doesn't speak any English. He knows numbers, though.

What *does* he say? asked Pete. The idea had really tickled him.

I cleared my throat. I knew I couldn't do it right, like the Martian did it, but I tried anyway. I tried to sort of sing it like the Martian did.

He says, I said, sherrit nek hazzer minny most.

I would like to go home now, said Pete Law.

My father blinked.

What do you mean? he asked Pete. Will you not have another drink?

Pete waved his hands.

No no. That's what *she* said. That's what her Martian said. Her Martian speaks Magyar. Who'd have thought? Either that, he added, or the goddamn kids have got a goddamn Hungarian cooped up in a shed someplace.

He laughed, and reached for his hat.

We'd better go, he said, and they both stood up.

A goddamn *what*? I said.

I sat on the harbourside by myself. I tried to find Mars in the sky. The stars looked different here than they had on the doorstep, when my father had pointed at Mars and told me about the canals and Panic and Fear.

I touched my eyebrow with one fingertip. It was still sore.

I'd showed them where the wormy blue door was but I'd waited outside because I didn't want to see him again. The Martian, or whatever he was. It was me that'd got him beat up, so I'd figured he wouldn't want to see me, anyway. Through the door I'd heard them talking. I'd listened for a little while — it *was* like singing, or maybe like a vaudeville show where the guys talk backwards or something – but then I went away. I went home. An hour later my father came home, too.

He hugged me. My father always smelled very clean, like soap. He kissed me on my hair, right where the parting is. Then he poured himself a glass of the clear stuff, and then he poured me one, too, and I took it, even though I don't much care for boozing. We both sat down at the table.

Mr Law's mother, he said, was born in Budapest. Budapest, he said, is in Hungary.

I nodded.

Okay, I said.

Mr Law, he said, was able to speak with Laszlo Szengeller.

Okay, I said again. I sipped my drink. I don't know what it was. It stung my lips. Then I said: who the hell is Laszlo Szengeller?

Laszlo Szengeller, my father said, is the greatest mathematician in Europe, and it turned out that he did think it was funny, or at least a little funny, after all, because he smiled.

Okay, I said.

He is your Martian, my father said.

Okay, I said.

It turned out that this Szellenger had come to New York on a Norddeutscher Lloyd liner, just like anyone might. There was a meeting or convention of math brains up at Morningside Heights. Analytic number theory, my father said. This Szellenger was the guest of honour. Only he hadn't showed up: this Szellenger, my father said, was one of these guys who's a whiz in math and science but can't do up his own shoelaces. Szellenger got lost as he left the piers. Sometime in the night the poor dummy jaywalked out into Pearl Street and got knocked flat by a car. That's where Johnny found him.

Isn't that just like Johnny. Just like Johnny and goddamn Joe Gillray. They find the smartest guy in Europe just sitting in the street, and the best thing they can think to do with him is put him in a booth at goddamn Coney Island.

There is no need to be embarrassed, my father said, and touched my cheek with the back of his hand. Mr Szellenger is perfectly well now, he said, and smiled. Mr Law told me that he said to say hello to you. Hello and goodbye.

That was when I came down to the harbourside to sit by myself. I couldn't find Mars. Everything up there looked alike to me. Everything down here too.

Until now we haven't published any translated fiction, but when Miha Mazzini's story arrived while I was actually reading his novel The German Lottery *(published by CB Editions), I had to take it as a sign.*

'I'm The One' was translated from Slovenian by Maja Visenjak.

I'm the One
Miha Mazzini

I'm the one who called just now. I got the fax machine and at first I wanted to put down the phone, but then I thought about the machine on the other end of the line, wanting to communicate with me. A twirling tone, like spaghetti round a fork. I was touched by the helplessness of a machine that could not talk, and of me, incapable of communicating.

That is probably why I decided to make an audio recording of this letter and attach it to an email. A few times <#-#-#-#-#-#-#> I apologise, but I will keep interrupting this and re-recording, and as I'm not very good with the mouse, the recording may not be spliced together very well.

I know how busy you are. You can listen to this in instalments.

Your mother died alone. I was going to erase that, as there is no other way of dying, but I had always thought there was a special bond between us. Thirty years is a long time and you probably imagine it as a straight line, but living together is not like that; there are twists, oscillations, barriers, jumps. Perhaps no life is a straight line; even if I look at my own, or you at yours. You're still younger than our marriage was.

I don't want to keep you. I'll only tell you what I failed to mention in the previous letters. I tried to write this time, too, but I couldn't. It'll be easier for me to speak, as I seem to have had more and more inner conversations with you over the last year. Probably more than we ever talked in reality.

You were quick even at birth, you simply fell into the doctor's hands. And just as at the age of two you rejected the porridge I'd made for you with a single, very final NO, you rejected everything we <#-#-#-#-#-#-#> Don't get me wrong, I don't want to reproach you. That's just what you're like. It was the right thing to do, going to America, and I'm proud that you have your own successful company. I can imagine how boring our life must have seemed to you when you were still in school. You went to Italy in grade three, to do the international baccalaureate. On your own. I was worried, but at the same time I admired you. I digress again. Back to your mother. She went to the doctor's and came back separated from me. Enveloped in an invisible cocoon. There was no change in what she said; if we were corresponding, like you and me, I wouldn't have noticed anything. She pushed me away somehow, as if she'd moved to another apartment. I left her alone for a couple of days before I started asking questions. No, everything was alright, she said.

I went to see the doctor, we both had the same one, and I didn't know what to say, but then she asked: 'How is your wife taking it?' I replied with something vague and then I figured out the diagnosis.

Your mother went for chemotherapy once a month, her hair fell out, she was sick, all the things you see in movies and read about in magazines, but with the addition of the smells and sensations; how cold her skin felt in those brief moments before she withdrew from me. She never mentioned her illness and I acted to the very end as if nothing was happening. She moved to your room and locked herself in. I admit I eavesdropped and then fled to the bathroom whenever she cried. At other times there was a sort of mumbling, I didn't know what it could be. When a taxi came to take her for chemotherapy, I dug out the spare key from the basement and went into her room. Pictures of Jesus and Mary, a rosary.

You flew in for the funeral, you know everything about that, but later I had to clear her things by myself. I threw it all in the dumpster or gave it to charity. The only things I didn't know what to do with were the religious pictures. In the end, I turned them to face the wall in your room; the only thing left was the furniture.

I wished I could have a job at least partly like yours: according to what you write and I imagine, it involves meeting after meeting, decision after decision, from morning till night. You know that in Slovenia the head of a division in a big state owned company has much too much time to think during working hours. And that I'm not so high on the hierarchical ladder as to sit behind a door you cannot see through, but am in an important enough position for my monitor to be turned away from those passing by. I'll never forget how you came to visit me when you were still in elementary school and asked with astonishment: 'And you sit here? For eight hours? Just sitting?'

At home I photographed an Italian language coursebook and transferred the photographs to the computer at work and every time I learnt an irregular verb, I nodded in satisfaction so that my subordinates could see that I was doing something.

I know how much you detested our way of doing things and how much you wanted to go to America. Did it fulfil your hopes?

I don't want to defend myself, but I would like to remind you of that afternoon when you came home from your first day at your first job when you were a student, totally in shock: the other employees sat you in a chair and told you not to do any work because that would raise their norm. If everyone cooperated and the norm was set low enough, people were able to go home rested and be ready to do some real work for themselves in the afternoon.

Are you happy in America? Well, I know employers everywhere want your body, but at that time I so wanted mine to take my soul too, at least for eight hours, the days seemed so very long.
<#-#-#-#-#-#>

Anyway, what was I going to say? I wanted to go to the Monday morning meetings, but then suffered every time as I watched my boss making the wrong decisions. He had been in that position for four years but it would have been more useful for the company if he had spent the time learning to play the mouth organ. The heads of divisions left the meetings exhausted and went directly to the canteen for coffee, spending a long time blowing ripples over the top before finishing with small sips. The predominant opinion was that behind our boss's hopelessness lay a cunning plan: the chief executive wanted to privatise the company and so had appointed idiots in the directorial positions who would ruin everything and pave the way for a cheap buyout.

And then one afternoon I bumped into the chief executive himself in the corridor. He was alone, without his usual entourage of secretaries, assistants, and assorted brown-nosers. 'How are you?' he asked me in haste as we shook hands — he was already looking at the elevator doors. If your mother had been alive and you still dependent on me, I would have kept quiet. In the past, every moment at work, I was aware of having to support you two, that I wasn't keeping quiet for myself. Don't get me wrong, I'm not re<#-#-#-#-#-#-#> At first he looked at me in surprise as I talked and talked. Then he began listening in astonishment, shaking his head, no, there was no plan, he was not going to buy the company. He almost ran to the elevator, shouting over his shoulder that his secretary would give me an appointment.

I went to the office and learned the verb *accorgere*. I've never had much personal stuff there, so I wasn't afraid of packing.

The chief executive's PA called and gave me an appointment. I wondered if I should get a new suit, but then decided to wear the one I bought for your mother's funeral. The chief executive gave me a whole hour of his time and, with the exception of the greeting, spent the entire time apologising. Not specifically, but in a roundabout, fuzzy manner, the way politicians do. Every word clear but combined into a long series of puffs, as if emitted by the exhaust pipe of an old car running on honey. The gist of it was that politicians dictated who he employed and that he had to carefully ensure that members of all the key political parties were equally represented. That's why he got who he got. And anyway, he had never been interested in the field our company was involved in, he had done something entirely different at university. And so on.

At home, I sat in the kitchen, holding a cup of tea in my hands until it went cold. Can you still remember how dull November is in Ljubljana?

All that went through my head was: there is no plan. The chief executive was where he was because he could not be anywhere else. Other directors were there because they knew the right people. They were appointed to positions of ineptitude by their connections and I by my obedience. When I thought about what an expert I'd been an <#-#-#-#-#-#-#> Enough, I don't want to go on about it. What I'd like to tell you is that I abandoned my Italian and thought about the horrible void that gaped before me. I didn't just sleep on it, but spent a whole week obsessing about it, increasingly numbed by the horror of our fate being in the hands of people who were totally inept. No big plan. No great mind behind it all. Not even a secret organization. Nothing. Our bosses were idiots playing their small, insignificant games, tripping over one another while trying to climb higher. We were at a court of intrigue, but the king was not only invisible, he wasn't there at all.

I spent the weekend sitting on a kitchen chair, brewing gallons of tea. After a few pots of Ceylon, my heart began palpitating, so I switched to herbal. All I could see through the window was fog swirling in thick, sticky threads.

I decided to sell the apartment and move to a smaller one. To leave my job and <#-#-#-#-#-#-#> On Sunday I changed my mind and copied the German language coursebook with my camera.

As you know, it then took nearly six months before I really sold the apartment. The last things I removed were the religious pictures. I swallowed hard and focused on my right hand before opening the door to your room. It was stuffy and dusty and the wind occasionally swept the window with fallen cherry tree petals. I waited, followed one petal all the way to the window, watched it swirling there until it helplessly succumbed and the wind carried it away. I didn't know and to this day haven't recognised the burden that was weighing on me. In my left hand, I was holding an open biodegradable bag, gathering strength. My hand paused just before reaching the pictures, but the memories didn't come until I turned the images around and saw the pure, lively colors. It was worth it, is all I can say. If my life seems boring to you, with her and with <#-#-#-#-#-#-#> I stood in the middle of the kitchen, holding the bag. The picture frames knocked against each other gently whenever my arm shook. She had never been a believer, never mentioned God. But after she got ill, she exchanged me for him. She addressed all her requests and questions to Him who has a carefully woven plan for us all. Then she died and I believed in him no more than I had before.

I chose my oldest suit, wrapped the bag in it, and took it to a Christian charity collection point.

The next year, nothing changed at work — i.e., things kept going downhill. Whenever I met friends from university or acquaintances in my field, they all moaned about how badly they were doing, but in the end winked, implying that those up there had a plan. The world economic crisis began and companies fell like dominoes. No one bought them out and all the employees who'd been laid off went out on the streets with empty cardboard boxes. I read *Faustus* in German, translating word by word, then Dante in Italian, and in the meantime followed the news on the Internet, where all the debates revolved around conspiracy theories, the plans of secret networks and the great mind behind it all. There was a smell of war in the air.

One lunchtime, a young employee took the seat opposite me in the canteen and we began chatting. After the cursory polite introductions, he steered the conversation in the direction of secret plans, and I don't know what was up with him, but he paused in mid-sentence, and looked at me for a long time. Then he said:

'This is going to sound strange, but the other day, as I listened to the boss, it struck me, what if he's just stupid and incapable? And not just him, but all of them? What if there is no plan behind it all and this is just a ship of fools?'

I kept shaking my head, comforting him. He could no longer see me, focused on his thoughts, staring into space.

'My girlfriend tells me we should take a loan for a house, but...
But how can I have children in a world like this?'

'I'm the one,' I said.

He choked out a few more sentences before stopping and
looking at me with surprise:

'Which one?'

'The one behind it all, with a plan.'

'But... you're just a head of —'

'True, but on purpose. You know yourself that those at the
top come and go; they're always in the public eye. It's safer lower
down. You mustn't tell anyone though.'

'I won't,' he promised fervently. 'So there is a plan?'

'For this company, yes. I don't know about the rest. It's outside
my jurisdiction.'

'I see,' he said, nodding and winking. I returned the wink.

And that was that. Of course, he did tell others. I noticed that the
atmosphere in the company slowly improved. People became less
dejected and despondent. They protested less when the lay-offs
came; they knew they were just part of the plan. The older ones
went first — except me, no one ever talks to me. Sometimes they
come with a request concerning themselves or a relative, but I just
shake my head helplessly as if I don't know what they're talking
about. They resent it, but not as much as you would expect.
They know there's a Plan behind it all, which is beyond their
understanding, and that in this company I'm its caretaker and
implementer.

Ever since that talk in the canteen, I've been meaning to tell
you about this, but I didn't want to bother you. On the other
hand, it seems I've started something that should be spread wider.
You've always been like a cork out of a champagne bottle when
you tackle something. As I watched the American invasion of

Iraq on television, the collapse of the system, the plundering of the museums, I had the same feelings I'd had at those Monday morning meetings: they must have a plan, they must. It transpired they did not.

Whenever I see Iraq in the news, I remember this feeling, and you; America needs someone who'll take this responsibility onto themselves. You would know how to do it, you'd organise a network of older people, grey haired, fatherly, who in moments of general despair quietly ask their colleagues not to tell anyone about them being the one. *The one.* People cannot get by without a plan, without a purpose. Jesus tried to save the world with love and after over two millennia, we can safely say things have not worked out for the best. It's time to salvage the situation by taking responsibility.

That's all I wanted to tell you. You don't have to answer, just think about it. I must finish while the light is still good and I can photograph the Japanese language coursebook.

*I can't decide whether S R Mastrantone's story
is a reality check for a paedophobic nation, or an
idealistic fantasy. Perhaps it's a little of both.*

Just Kids

S R Mastrantone

It was one AM, and the kids were outside again.

Frank felt the muscles in his neck and abdomen tense as he
lay on his back in the darkness. At first he tried to ignore the
noise: bullish half-shouts in newly broken voices, occasionally
punctuated by high pitched, girlish laughter. He reached over to
the other side of the bed and pulled Sophie closer, being careful
not to press too hard against the bump in her belly; he pushed his
exposed ear against her back to block out the sound. But it found
a way through all the same.

He gave up trying to sleep and went over to the window. Most
of the street was visible through the net curtains but the kids were
standing out of sight at the foot of the building, three storeys
below. To see them he had to open the window, which he did as
quietly as possible.

There were five of them: three boys and two girls. One boy sat on a moped with L plates while the rest sat up against the wall of Frank's building.

Frank considered shouting something, telling them to clear off.

If it were the 1960s I would, he thought. Things, teenagers and men, had been made differently then. Now, it was different.

Though Frank could not attest directly to the veracity of the claim, having been born in the mid 1980s, those of his father's generation expressed the opinion repeatedly on talk radio.

And it was bad out there.

A lawyer had been stabbed by a gang of fourteen-year-olds at Camden tube station last year. That was just three miles away. Some of the kids had never been caught.

There was no guarantee that *these* kids weren't *those* kids.

Shouting would draw attention to himself. They would know where he lived.

He shut the window and another round of laughter rose up from below. He hoped they hadn't seen him.

Frank got back into bed but didn't lie down; instead he sat up against the wall with only his legs beneath the covers.

There was always the police. Perhaps a bit strong to begin with. What about community support officers? He could say he was concerned for the welfare of his elderly neighbour, rather than his own.

'They're just kids,' is what Sophie would say, and in the past he would have agreed; back when the kids were turning up sporadically. But three times in a week was too much. Something needed to be done.

On his way home from work the next day, he stopped at the Poundworld in the parade of shops next to the flat. He found a bag of earplugs at the very back of the shop but another, more colourful bag nearby grabbed his attention:

WATER BALLOON BUMPER FUN PACK

Frank took both bags to the counter.

Later that evening, he sat at the dinner table with a beer. Sophie was opposite him reading a copy of the day's *Metro* that Frank had brought back with him from his commute.

'What did you get?' Sophie asked looking at the Poundworld bag hanging on the back of Frank's chair.

His mind began to search for a lie but his pause was too long. 'Ear plugs and water balloons. I'm going to drop the balloons on those kids if the ear plugs don't work. Or maybe I'll drop them anyway'

'Oh good. That sounds like a great idea. Let me know how that goes.' She shook her head and looked back down at the paper.

He searched for a witty riposte but again, too much time passed. Instead, he said: 'I will,' and went upstairs to put the bag under their bed.

They came back two days later. Friday night.

It was the engine of the moped that woke him and the shouting that kept him awake. Why couldn't they just talk? It would be fine if they just talked.

In the mess of voices he could occasionally pick out something meaningful, a swear word or something to do with sex.

Slowly, he rolled onto his stomach and reached under the bed for the bag. Sophie stirred. 'Frank?'

He made his voice sound sleepy. 'Yeah.'

'You okay?'

'Yes. Just rolling over.' His hand found its target.

'Don't bother them. They'll be gone in a minute.'

He pulled his hand back reluctantly and rolled over again to hug her. 'I wasn't going to. I just wanted to get my ear plugs.'

He had to wait two weeks to use the balloons.

Sophie's sister asked Sophie to visit her in Cornwall. She had been arguing with her alcoholic boyfriend, and they were on the verge of splitting up for the second time since Christmas.

'You don't mind being on your own?' Sophie asked.

'Not at all. If I had any leave left I'd come too.'

She left on Thursday night. On the way home from work on Friday, Frank stopped at Poundworld to pick up a four pack of Czech beer, which he finished while watching *Lethal Weapon 3*. As he lay in bed at midnight, he heard laughter from out on the street. They were early.

Frank got up and opened the window. There were only two of them and they stood against the wall smoking, their mopeds up on kickstands. The kids were directly beneath Frank.

He listened to their conversation. One of them thought 'Carly' was a slag, while the other thought she was a laugh. They both agreed she was 'F to F' which Frank had a good idea meant the girl was attractive.

Not long after, another helmeted spectre pulled off the road and joined them. This one stayed on his moped and kept the sputtering little engine running. Frank waited for them to realise they might be making a bit too much noise, but all that happened was the kid on the bike took off his helmet to make himself at home. All the better to soak his head.

He had seen enough. He retrieved the Poundworld bag from under the bed and with slightly drunken enthusiasm, pulled the seam of the bag. The cheap plastic split too readily. Balloons fell to the floor in all directions. He picked up three and went to the bathroom. The first balloon he filled was red and Frank was pleased with the way the end clung to the tap so that he didn't have to hold it in place. It swelled like fruit filmed by a time-lapse camera.

When all three were full, he carefully navigated his way to the window and peered out again. The three kids were stood in a huddle around the moped belonging to the most recent arrival, just three feet away from the wall of Frank's building.

It was too perfect. They were right below the window.

With the ends of all three balloons clasped between the fingers of his right hand, Frank leaned out of the window as far as he could and tossed the balloons underarm. Then in the same movement he pulled the window shut with his left hand and ducked down beneath the sill.

He waited; nothing happened.

For a long while all Frank could hear was his own excited heart in his ears. Eventually he heard muttering voices, followed shortly after by the pathetic gunning of the three bikes' engines. They were leaving!

Frank stood back up and watched as all three of the bikes drove off the curb and on to the road. They all turned left and vanished out of sight.

Had he won?

He opened the window and looked down. From the marks on the concrete below, it wasn't clear if the balloons had hit their target; but what did it matter? The effect had been the same.

Frank *had* won.

It wasn't until later, as sleep was coming in and the alcohol was beginning to be processed by his body, that it occurred to him that if the kids really were dangerous, he might have just started something he couldn't finish.

The next morning, Frank heard a strange metallic clacking coming from outside. When he opened the window and looked down he saw ten kids all sat up against the wall watching another kid trying to do tricks on a skateboard. Each time the kid fell, the board struck the pavement noisily.

In the light, the kids appeared younger.

They might even have been different kids. Frank wasn't sure, but he didn't think it mattered in the general scheme of his war. He promptly filled four balloons and dropped them out of the window. This time he heard a few squeals and shouts which made him smile.

After a late breakfast, Frank went shopping. Their neighbour, Mrs Hardy, was bent over picking something up by the wall where the kids had been earlier.

'Hello, Mrs Hardy,' Frank said. 'Everything okay?'

'Look at this,' she said and held out the remains of his water balloons on her palm. 'They're everywhere. I don't know what they are but how hard can it be to walk over to the bin?'

'It's these kids. They've been waking me up at night, you know. Have you heard them?'

'I've not heard anything,' she said. 'But my ears aren't what they used to be. It's this that bothers me.' She trowelled at the air with her outstretched palm to return his attention to the rubber shrapnel. 'I don't think they're biodegradable, you know.'

With a concerned shake of his head, he left Mrs Hardy to contemplate his mess. When he came back an hour later she had been replaced with three boys who leaned against the wall to Frank's building. He assumed they were boys, but all of them had the hoods of their sports tops pulled up over their heads so it was hard to tell. One of them dropped his hood and leered at him. Frank looked away quickly. Did he know?

Not wanting them to see where he lived (just in case), he kept walking past the alley that would have taken him to the entrance to his building. At the bushes that marked the end of the shops, he counted to sixty and walked back to his building, where he slipped down the alley unnoticed.

Sophie was due back on Wednesday. He missed her, had bought her flowers on sale at the florist next to Poundworld, but when they spoke on Tuesday evening he encouraged her to stay another night.

'You're being sensible, your sister is being an idiot,' he said to her over the phone. As he spoke he peered out of the bedroom window. 'If his temperature is that high he needs to go to the out-of-hours clinic. You should stay. It sounds like she needs you more than I do.'

'Are you sure?'

'Trust me. I've got everything under control.'

'Really?' She waited a moment before saying, 'How are your kids? Did you get to play with your balloons?'

'Everything is under control.'

Only that was a lie. The kids had been back every night since he first threw the balloons. Sometimes there had just been two, at other times there had been more than five. But whatever the arrangement, he realised he couldn't keep throwing balloons. They would become wise to it, if they hadn't already. They would see him. They would spray paint the door or post dog excrement through his letter box. Or worse. He had read in that day's *Metro* that some kid in an Eeyore mask had put a petrol bomb through an old lady's door in Dorset.

And this wasn't Dorset. This was London. They made kids differently here.

He needed a new plan; one that would solve the problem before Sophie came home. His mind kept returning to the kid that leered at him: had he known?

After their phone conversation, he drank more Czech beer and mulled on the gently mocking tone in her voice. Had there been something else in there too? Perhaps a little bit of genuine sympathy. Whatever it had been, he didn't like being felt sorry for.

He could piss in the balloons? They did sort of resemble tiny condoms, He could just attach one to... Or he could boil the kettle, put a bit of hot water in there to make them think it was piss?

Why not just scald them? They wouldn't come back then.

He took the empty beer bottle to the kitchen and put it in a plastic bag with the other empties. They clinked together melodiously.

Frank had an idea. He took the bag of bottles and a hammer from the kitchen drawer into the bedroom where he wrapped the bottles up in a duvet.

Much later, when the passing cars on the street were down to less than one a minute, he descended from the flat, slunk down the alley and began to sprinkle tiny pieces of glass on the pavement three stories below his bedroom window.

He was eating breakfast when he heard a scream. What were they doing now?

Frank went to the bedroom window and looked out.

Mrs Hardy was sitting on the pavement below, clutching her left leg. A smear of something dark coloured the concrete next to her.

'Can somebody help me?' The waver in her voice was audible even through the glass. He opened the window to get a better look.

That wasn't balloon water.

'I'm coming down,' he said.

By the time he got downstairs, she had been helped to a nearby bench by a group of concerned passers by, one of whom was a man in a suit talking to the emergency services on a mobile phone. Another woman sat on the bench with her arm across Mrs Hardy's shoulder.

'Mrs Hardy, what happened?' Frank asked, already knowing the answer.

'It's those begging... those *bloody* kids.' She spat the swear word out as if it had been stuck in her throat for a long time and she was glad to be rid of it. 'Look what they've done.'

She lifted her left foot. A semicircle of glass, the bottom of a bottle, stuck out of her shoe, the tip of a morbid iceberg.

Frank felt blood rushing to his face, trying to give him away. It was only meant to burst their tyres.

'Yes. Those kids. Something needs to be done,' Frank said.

Mrs Hardy nodded her trembling head.

The pavement had been cleared of glass by the time Frank came home from work.

He knocked on Mrs Hardy's door. She answered wearing a dressing gown and a foot bandage. The hospital wanted her back in the morning to remove more glass but other than that she was fine.

'I had a right limp already,' she said. 'Maybe now I'll balance.'

'Are you going to speak to the police?' Frank asked.

'The police? What about?'

'The kids, the ones that left the glass.'

'Oh. No, do you think I should?'

Yes, Frank did think she should. He'd thought so all day. It was the perfect way to end it all, make it a police matter. 'You don't know who you're dealing with these days, Mrs Hardy,' he said. 'But if you told the police they might be able to issue an anti-social behaviour order or something.'

'Surely the police don't need to get involved. I'd prefer to give them a piece of my mind. Maybe *you* can have a word with them? If you see them.'

'Trouble is,' he said to Sophie as they lay in bed that night, 'she's from a generation where it was acceptable to clip a kid round the ear if they misbehaved. She'll get her throat cut if she tries that now.'

Sophie sighed. It was threatening to become an argument. He'd jumped on her too quickly with it all, not allowed her to settle back in and share her news with him first. He regretted the bottle of wine he'd drunk before she walked through the door. 'Don't the police need a crime to have been committed?' Her voice was low and soft, the tone almost professional, like a priest listening to a particularly challenging confession. She lay on her back with her eyes closed, Frank's hand resting on the bump in her belly.

He took back the hand. 'What, like littering? That's a crime, isn't it? Or how about disturbing the peace? If I stood outside someone's window every night making noise at all hours...'

'They're kids. Didn't you ever stay our late and get drunk when you were that age?' But she already knew that answer and the words lost power as the question went along.

'I don't think you understand. It's because you don't read the news; if you read the news you'd know how they...'

'You're right, I am incredibly stupid, Frank. And you know what? All this is making my feeble brain hurt. So if you don't mind, I think I might go to sleep.'

'I didn't mean you were stupid. I just meant... it's not like when we were kids... Or like it was in the sixties...'

But it was too late. The cause was lost.

After their argument, Frank couldn't sleep. No matter how much he rolled around he couldn't get comfortable. His anger oppressed him from all sides like an inescapably hot summer night.

He wanted to wake her and explain it all again, now that he was starting to sober up.

They came just after one in the morning. He heard them coming, the rapid puttputtputt of their engines getting louder and louder until it was right below the window. His chest was tight and grew tighter as the shouting began. Two male voices locked into an argument for nearly ten minutes. Frank went to leave the bed but Sophie's hand moved across him and she pulled him toward her.

'They'll be gone in a minute,' she whispered and kissed his neck.

He stroked her head in return and waited for her to sleep. By the time her breathing was at the right, telltale pace, the kids were revving their engines.

Were they competing to be the loudest?

At the window he waited. The noise kept coming. His bladder was full and he contemplated emptying it over the kids' heads. But it was beyond that now. It had gone beyond practical jokes.

He moved quietly to the kitchen and then to the bathroom. After relieving himself, he went back into the kitchen just as the kettle boiled. Taking great care not to spill a drop on himself — he had filled it above the little plastic line — Frank took the boiling water to the bedroom and opened the window slowly and quietly. He looked down at the tops of three heads. One kid sat on a moped, one stood to the left of the bike and the other was crouching down by the back wheel. All were in pouring distance.

The kid sitting on the bike roared with laughter at something one of the other two had said.

'Go, go, go,' the crouched kid yelled and the kid on the moped began to rev the engine.

Frank held the kettle out of the window and took aim.

A shrill voice cut through the night. Frank nearly dropped the kettle.

'Could you shut up please, there's people trying to sleep.'

Frank pulled the kettle back inside and looked over to his right. Mrs Hardy was leaning out of her window.

The kids all looked up and Frank pulled further back out of sight.

'It's one in the flippin' morning. Don't you have homes to go to?' Her voice cracked slightly. It sounded as if it hadn't been raised in quite some time.

Frank waited for the abusive comeback and the swear words to fly. Instead a rather meek voice said: 'Sorry. We didn't know. His bike's broke and... We were just fixing it.'

'Sorry,' another voice added. There was some restrained laughter followed by the sound of a window closing.

Frank watched the three kids come into view from his vantage point a step back from the window. Their heads were down as they quietly wheeled their mopeds away from the building and out onto the road.

He sat watching twenty-four hour news for a long time. He saw a story about a young father who had been stabbed outside his house for confronting a gang of hooded youths who were sitting on his garden wall. Then he saw it again. And again.

It wasn't until the water had gone cold that Frank realised he was still holding the kettle. Outside it was getting light. When he climbed back into bed Sophie didn't stir. She could sleep through anything.

He put his hand on her bump and slept.

This is Colin Corrigan's second appearance in our anthology series: his story 'The Romantic' featured in All These Little Worlds. *His work also appears regularly in* The Stinging Fly.

Wonders of the Universe

Colin Corrigan

Wonders of the Universe is a television programme on BBC Two. It follows a fella called Brian Cox as he goes around the world spouting about science with a big happy head on him. Edel's sister bought her the series on DVD, and we started watching it, me and Edel, because Marilyn asked us to do more things together. Edel would have preferred to watch her *Grey's Anatomy* box set again, and I'd suggested pulling the dartboard out of the wardrobe so we wouldn't just be goggling at the telly, but we compromised. That was another thing Marilyn asked us to do.

We put the first episode on that Monday evening, the first week in November. I'd done a stocktake in the shop earlier, and I was just after my dinner, and her brain shuts down if you try to draw a map to the post office, never mind start charting galaxies, so I expected us both to be asleep after about five minutes. But to be honest, it was very good. Your man Cox is brilliant at explaining things, at making you think about stuff you wouldn't normally think about.

Like the way time is measured by change. I couldn't help looking around our living room, Edel on her side of the couch, me on mine, trying to spot the differences between now and this time last year, or two years ago.

And how things can break on their own, but they almost never fix themselves.

And, when you look at it from the outside, the whole universe is basically an explosion in super super slow motion, and it will one day just spread out, cool down, and stop. Then there will be literally nothing going on.

'That was amazing, wasn't it?' said Edel, turning down the credits.

'What's amazing me is that there wasn't a word out of you for nearly an hour.'

She shrugged, and pouted her lips, and drew a two-inch diagonal across the top of her chest with her finger. In our early days she would perform that signal in the pub, or the car, or my mother's kitchen. I remember her doing it at Derek Cassidy's funeral.

'I haven't seen that in a while,' I said.

And then we took some more of Marilyn's advice, right there on the couch.

To be honest, it was Edel's sister's idea, the counselling. Until Edel first brought it up, I didn't know she talked to her sister about our relationship problems. I wasn't even sure we had relationship problems, exactly. But they had already looked it up on the internet, and there was an Accord centre just over in Blanchardstown. And Edel had called and made an appointment for us and everything.

'Accord,' I said. 'Isn't that the Catholic crowd?'

'We're Catholic,' she said.

I snorted. And she said:

'You see, this is exactly what I'm talking about.'

'What is?'

'If you don't know yourself, there's no sense in me telling you.'

Marilyn is pushing sixty, I'd say, but she still dresses like a hippy. She paints her lips a deep purple colour, the same shade as the fringe of her poncho, her dangly earrings and her fingernails, which Edel says are fake. I had been expecting a nun.

In the sessions, she gets us to sit in a triangle. Marilyn asks the questions, and me and Edel direct our answers to each other. The first day, when it was my turn to talk, she asked me to describe a time when things were really good between us.

'Remember after your da died,' I said.

Edel breathed in and wrapped her bottom lip over her little moustache, put her head back at an angle and glared at me down the length of her nose.

'That's the look I'm talking about,' I said to Marilyn.

'I think she's wondering why you chose this moment to mention her father's passing.'

'I'm just saying, after her da died we used to go around to his house and fix the place up.'

'Tell Edel what you remember about it.'

I thought back to the first time she brought me round there. We weren't married that long then, maybe six or eight months. Her father had been up in St Doolagh's hospice since before we met, and the house had been lying idle. The electricity was cut off. Edel led me through the rooms and hallways, pointing out the mantelpiece she fell against when she was seven, the chair she found her mother dead in, the shed at the end of the garden that used to house the toilet. Standing in the bedroom she shared with her sister for twenty-four years, she started to cry.

She had plans to do the place up so she could rent it out, and I described the different ways I could help her. We talked about extending into the back garden, putting in a new kitchen, converting the attic into a bedroom. The low spring sun blazed through the filthy, timber-framed, single-glazed windows at the back of the house. It caught in her hair and made it look reddish, almost blonde.

'It was an absolute state,' I said.

'Try to think of something positive,' said Marilyn.

'I didn't mean it like that,' I said. 'I liked it... how much there was to be done.'

I turned back to Edel.

'Remember how the floorboards in the living room were rotten under that mangy auld carpet? And the wallpaper in the hall peeling off the damp?'

'Yeah?' said Edel.

'I don't know,' I said. 'It was sort of... exciting.'

We did a great job on that house. We got lads in to put down the foundations for the extension and lay the blocks, but I did the roofing and all the plastering and that myself. I rewired the whole house, mounted wall lights, downlighters and uplighters, fitted the kitchen and two new en suites. Edel helped out a good bit too. She picked out the furniture and the kitchen press doors, and she did some of the painting herself as well. Every weekend and most evenings for a year and a half we were there laying tiles, varnishing floorboards, hanging doors.

When it was finished, we found some improvements to make on our own apartment, but that was brand new when we bought it, and most things worked fine. We tried to have a baby for a while, until we found out about her ovaries. We spent two weeks in Marbella, which was excellent, beaches and sun and cocktails and massages and everything. Then we came home.

There was a lot of interest in the place when we advertised it on the internet, and we offered it to a group of four girls from Tipperary. They were friends from school, they were all working, and they seemed to have heads on their shoulders, so we didn't think they'd be too much trouble.

One of them though, Angela, was laid off by Quinn Insurance, and I had to drive over there to drop off a few forms for her rent allowance.

Angela answered the door in her dressing gown, her hair wrapped up in a towel.

'I'm sorry,' she said. 'I'm just out of the shower.'

'You're in the room with the the Triton Aspirante, aren't you?'

'The what?'

'It's a powerful shower.'

She laughed and asked me in for a cup of tea, and I said, 'Why not?' She led me down the hall, through the open plan living and dining areas and into the urban oak kitchen. I like being in that house. No matter which way I turn my head, I can see something that I fixed.

As Angela was boiling the kettle, I noticed a few drops of water on the kitchen floor, under the skylight.

'Oh yeah,' she said, 'that happens sometimes. It's never too bad though.'

'Jesus,' I said, 'I'd better take a look at that.'

I went out to the back garden, got the ladder from the side of the house and climbed up on the roof. I was thinking that maybe one of the tiles was cracked. They'd had Sky in installing a satellite dish a few weeks before, and a lot of those fellas are absolute chancers. But I couldn't right away see what was causing the leak. I ran my thumb along where the window frame joins with the roof, looking for a gap in the sealing.

Right underneath me, Angela sat down at the kitchen table, put her foot up on the other chair, and began to rub Johnson's Baby Lotion into her leg.

'Jesus,' I said. Surely she had heard me setting the ladder against the wall, my steps on the roof. She must have sensed my shadow, which was falling across her lifted knee and shin. She knows I'm a married man.

And I'm not the sort of fella who plays around all the time. I hadn't cheated on Edel since my stag.

And to be honest, of the four girls living in the house, Angela is the least good looking. Her face is too big for her eyes, one of her front teeth is too big for her mouth. Generally speaking, she's too big. But from where I knelt against the wind looking down into the yellow warmth of the kitchen, her thigh looked smooth and soft as she squeezed it between her fingers.

I did my best to be quiet going down the ladder. I stood with my back to the wall for at least five minutes. When I went in she was still sitting there with her foot up on the chair. Her robe draped down either side of her bare knee, and hung low enough across her chest to show off the gap where her tits start to spread apart.

'Your tea's cold,' she said. 'I'll stick on a fresh brew?'

Jesus no. I told her I needed silicone for the window, that I'd be back tomorrow or the next day to seal it.

I got two penalty points for speeding on my way back to the shop.

I work in an electrical supply and repair shop on the North Circular Road. If you need a hose for your Hoover or a basket for your fryer we'll get you sorted. And we fix anything from toasters to washing machines. We've been booming since the recession, nobody being as quick anymore when their dishwasher breaks down to just go out and buy a new one.

Most mornings I go out on house calls and deliveries, then I spend the afternoons in the shop. The day after I discovered the leak in the skylight, my boss asked me to go for a pint with him after we closed up for the evening.

'I don't know, Mick,' I said. 'I've the car with me.'

'Marilyn not approve of your going for a pint with the lads?'

'It's not that,' I said, wondering why I ever told him about the marriage counselling.

Kenny, Mick's son who works in the shop after school, stuck his head out of the storeroom.

'He must be off to lash it into that fat tenant of his again.'

'What do you mean, again?' I said. 'I haven't laid a finger on her.'

'I have a proposition for you,' said Mick. 'You'll want to hear it.'

I went for one shandy, and Mick laid out his plan. He had rented another, larger premises over on the Southside, and was planning on opening it after Christmas. He wanted me to take over running the existing shop.

'But who'll do the repair round?' I said.

'We'll get someone else in.'

I pictured myself spending whole days doing the books and writing up orders.

'You know the shop inside out already,' he said. 'And you're good with the customers.'

'A dab hand with the ladies, lately,' said Kenny.

'And there's a raise in it for you,' said Mick.

'That'll come in handy when your wife issues the divorce,' said Kenny.

'She's not going to divorce me,' I said.

'Don't mind him,' said Mick. 'Have you seen the one he's going around with now? Flat as a pancake.'

'What one?' I said.

'Remember she was hanging around the shop on Friday?'

'Was that a girl?' I said, and Mick sprayed the table with half-chewed bits of crisps.

I hadn't even thought of that. Divorce.

We watched the second episode of *Wonders of the Universe*. This one was about how we're all made from the elements, carbon and oxygen and what have you, that were formed millions of years ago inside exploding stars. We didn't even make it to the end of the programme before Edel nibbled my ear.

I was a bit nervous, asking her to get her Johnson's Baby Lotion, but she didn't blink. She rubbed it into her thighs and stomach and tits, then into my balls and my cock, and I almost forgot about Angela. The sex, when we got around to it, was even better than episode one's.

Afterwards, I came back from the toilet and found the bed empty. Edel was lying on the couch in the living room, two minutes into the next programme. I squeezed in beside her and she put her feet on my lap. This one was about gravity, and Cox got strapped into a giant centrifuge that spun him round and round until he experienced a gravitational force five times stronger than normal. The skin on his face sagged down under his eyes and cheekbones like a zombie's, and his bottom lip drooped onto his chin, exposing his teeth. Edel laughed and laughed. Then he tried to explain Einstein's

Theory of Relativity, and to be honest I found all that stuff about warped spacetime hard to get my head around. I was very tired.

But I couldn't sleep, thinking about that leak in the skylight. The forecast was for rain. I got up three times during the night to piss.

I called over the next afternoon to take another look at it. I would have waited until evening, when there was more chance one of the other girls would be home, but there wasn't much point in getting up on the roof in the dark. Katie, the little blonde one, answered the door. She was wearing her nurse's uniform.

Up on the roof, I brushed off the moss and muck from around the window frame and found a bit of wear on the seal which may have been allowing the water to seep through. I put a new layer of silicone over it and hoped it would do the trick.

Katie waved up at me through the window. The front door opened and slammed shut. I packed up as quick as I could, but when I went back in through the kitchen Angela was there in her dressing gown, combing her wet hair.

'You're getting good use out of that shower, anyway,' I said.

'It's strange,' she said, 'because I'm still a very dirty girl.'

Jesus. She asked me to have a look at the radiator in her bedroom, she said she had twisted the knob but she couldn't get it turned on.

Her room didn't feel cold, but it was hard to tell because I was already sweating anyway. There was a strong smell of lavender. I put my hand to the radiator and had to yank it away again, it was roasting. As I turned around, Angela pushed her dressing gown off her shoulders and it landed on the carpet behind her heels with a whisper. Her big round breasts and bigger, rounder belly were wrapped into a corset, her thighs were hooked up in suspenders, and Jesus, were they...? Yep, crotchless knickers.

'Hang on a minute,' I said, and I turned off my phone.

In the car on the way over to the Accord centre, Edel took a CD from her handbag and slotted it into the stereo. That old song 'Things Can Only Get Better' came on.

'Who is this again?' I said.

'D:Ream.'

'When did you start listening to these?'

'This was my favourite song when I was in sixth year.'

'Is it that old?'

She boxed me in the back of my head.

'It was re-released a few years later,' she said, 'when Tony Blair made it the anthem for New Labour.'

I looked at her.

'Do you buy many CDs?' I said.

'Sometimes.'

When we got inside and were sitting waiting at reception, I thought about how much things had already improved between us. The evenings together on the couch, the sex, now conversations about music and British politics. I was glad I'd warned Angela that what happened was only a once-off. When I wrote out the cheque for the next three sessions, I slipped a ten euro note into the envelope, as a tip.

Inside, we told Marilyn about how we had finished *Wonders of the Universe*.

'Science is very important,' she said. 'But we mustn't forget to pray.'

Edel came home late from work that Thursday, I think it was, with a Chinese and a new DVD.

'*Wonders of the Solar System*,' I said. 'Is this the sequel?'

She shook her head.

'The Solar System came before the Universe.'

I dished out the takeaway and brought it in to her on the couch. Cox drove into Death Valley and, using a thermometer, a tin can of water, and an umbrella, he calculated the total energy the sun emits every second.

'And that's why I love physics,' he said.

I pulled Edel's feet up onto my lap and rubbed her toes and the soles of her feet. I massaged her calves. I lifted her foot and put her little toe in my mouth. She kicked me away without turning her face from the screen.

'Are you alright?' I said.

She pointed her chin at the telly.

Jesus, I thought, maybe she knows about Angela.

I ran my hand up to her thigh.

'Sshh,' she said. 'I'm watching this.'

I waited until the programme was over.

'Right. I'm off to bed,' I said.

'Okay,' she said. She picked up the remote and started the next episode. I sat there for a minute wondering what to do.

Then she looked at me.

'Right,' I said. 'Night, so.'

Angela kept sending me texts. She needed someone to take a close look at her plumbing. There's something wrong with her mattress, it's not squeaking the way it should be. This sort of stuff. I had to make sure I didn't leave my phone lying around at home.

I drove over there, just to tell her to stop.

'You could ruin my marriage,' I said to her, standing in the hall. 'You could ruin my life.'

'I'm sorry,' she said, 'I won't do it again,' but even as she was saying that she reached out and cupped my balls in her hand.

'What are you doing?'

'What am I doing?' She zipped down my fly with her other hand.

'Well alright, then, but this is the very last time,' I said. 'I'm serious.'

I stayed late in work to try to get my head around the Quickbooks on the computer, and when I got home Edel was sitting by herself on the couch, with the lights off. Cox was going on about how Einstein's theory about gravity is so beautiful.

'We've already seen this,' I said.

'Yeah. It's one of my favourite episodes.'

I sat down beside her. All that stuff about the Theory of Relativity and warped spacetime wasn't making any more sense to me the second time round, so I picked up the laptop to check my emails.

Buy cheap flights in the sale at Ryanair.com. Inject a bit of Italian flair into your laundry room with the stylish Zanussi ZWG7140P washing machine. Angela O'Dwyer wants to be friends on Facebook. It took me a minute to cop on to who Angela O'Dwyer was. Then I panicked and slammed the screen shut.

I sneaked a glance at Edel, and my pulse slowed a bit when I saw her eyes were still gummed to the telly. I brought the laptop into the kitchen and sat at the table, facing the door.

'I knew I shouldn't have encouraged her,' I said.

I opened Angela's friend request and clicked on 'Ignore', then changed my Facebook settings to make it harder for people to track me down. I blocked her from my email account. I checked back through the browser's web history to delete any mention of her.

The BBC iPlayer search results for Brian Cox. The Brian Cox Wikipedia page. The @ProfBrianCox Twitter account. Interviews with Brian Cox on the *Telegraph*, *Guardian*, *Sun*, *Daily Mail*, *Hello Magazine*, and Sky News websites. An article called 'Brian Cox calls Ghost Believers Nobbers', another called 'TV scientist Brian Cox rejoins his old pop band D:Ream'. Dozens of Youtube clips of D:Ream concerts from the Nineties, with a young Brian Cox rocking away on the keyboards.

She had been looking at this stuff for an hour and a half that Tuesday, four hours that Wednesday, two spells totalling nearly seven hours that Thursday. The previous night she had been online between three in the morning and a quarter to six, when I was asleep in bed.

The Professor Brian Cox Appreciation page. Sue Rider Management, the 'talent representation for Dr Brian Cox'. Photographs of him and his wife, a TV presenter called Gia Milinovich, at different movie premieres and awards ceremonies, and at the beach. A bulletin board thread with dozens of comments about how their son George's middle name is Eagle, after the Apollo 11 lunar module, and how cool that is. Another about which playschool George is likely to be joining next September.

I stood up, careful not to scrape the chair's legs on the floor, snuck over and peered in through the gap in the living room door. I could only make out a general sense of her shape against the cushions. On the telly, they cut to a wide shot of Cox standing before a bright sunrise, and I saw Edel, sitting forward in the yellow glow, her eyes dull ponds of reflected light, her fingers shoved down inside her pyjama bottoms.

Driving over to the Accord centre for our next session, I wondered what the hell I was going to talk about. Edel had D:Ream on the radio again.

'Their other songs are nowhere near as good, are they?'

'You're right,' she said. 'They're nowhere near as good as all the songs you've written.'

She flipped down her sun visor and squinted at the little mirror. She looked different.

'Did you get your hair done?'

'Yesterday morning.'

'It's nice.'

'She took too much off,' she said, and slammed the visor up.

Marilyn got us to play charades.

'Now, Edel. You mime out something that you enjoyed doing this week, and then, Kevin, you have to guess what it was.'

Edel stood up, took Marilyn by the elbow, led her across the room and sat her in the chair behind her desk. Then she walked away, turned around, and went back and stood in front of the desk, moving her hands about in the air.

She stopped and looked at me. I looked at Marilyn. Marilyn looked at Edel.

She gasped, and stood up straight for a moment with a finger on her lips, thinking, or maybe pretending to think. Then she went and picked up her hand bag and pulled out a big hardback book with a close-up of a rainbow on the cover. She brought it back to the desk and opened it in front of Marilyn. Marilyn put on her reading glasses.

'Dear Edel, I hope you are as inspired by the myriad possibilities of the universe as I am. All the best, Brian.'

She picked up the book and looked at the cover.

'*The Quantum Universe, Everything That Can Happen Does Happen,* by Jeff Forshaw and Brian Cox... He signed his book for you?'

Edel nodded and rocked back on her heel like a six-year-old.

'He came to Eason's yesterday afternoon. You should have seen the amount of people there, the line went all the way out of the shop and halfway down Abbey Street. It was lucky I got there five hours early.'

'Wow,' said Marilyn.

'He was really really nice, really normal. He chatted away with everyone. I told him I'd seen all his TV programmes, like, five times already.'

She smiled down at Marilyn, then turned and smiled at me.

I looked at Marilyn.

'It's a lovely note he wrote,' said Marilyn.

'But then,' said Edel, 'the woman from Eason's led me away, because she said she had to keep the line moving.'

'I suppose there were a lot of people waiting,' said Marilyn.

'Yeah, but then the girl after me started telling him all about how she had just started college, and she was doing physics because she'd been inspired by him, and he talked to her for ages, and the Eason's woman didn't pull her away or even say anything to her, and then Brian got up and he... he... he hugged her.'

She covered her face with her hand and stood in the middle of the floor and shook. Every few seconds a soft sob escaped through her fingers. I looked at Marilyn. She stood up and went and put her arms around my wife.

'Hush, now,' she said.

I know it's kind of pathetic, getting all worked up like that over a celebrity. It's a small bit psycho, even. But I felt sorry for her. I hadn't seen her cry in a long time.

'To be honest,' I said, 'he's a bit of a wreck-the-head anyway.'

She took her hand away from her eyes and looked at me like I was the one who was cracked.

'He's so fucking happy all the time,' I said.

'But that's why I...'

I think she was going to say love, but she stopped herself.

'It's alright for him,' I said, 'with his dream job that flies him around to all these mad places, and he gets to experience zero gravity and fly faster than the speed of sound, and he's got his TV presenter wife and their kid called Eagle, and the royalties from his pop music career still flowing into his bank account. But the rest of us have more to worry about than the sun exploding.'

She wiped at her nose with the back of her hand, smearing snot across her cheek.

'You just don't understand,' she said.

And she's right. I don't understand. It's not that I've got no time for science. I'm a qualified electrician. But a lot of that stuff, when you think about it, just doesn't seem to matter. The wonders of the universe are out there, alright, but what most of us have to deal with every day is all the ordinary crap that surrounds us. Some stuff might look small or insignificant when you compare it to black holes and supernovas, but it seems bigger to us because it's closer. That's what I think, anyhow. Relativity or whatever has nothing to do with it.

A man came into the shop the next Monday and asked to speak to the manager.

'Mick isn't in today,' I said.

'The guy told me to ask for a Kevin.'

I remembered that I was the manager now.

'I'm Kevin,' I said.

He explained that Andy, our new repairs fella, had been around to his house that morning to have a look at his washing machine, which was leaking oil. Andy had stripped the washer and told the man that he needed a new transmission system, and reassembled it, and left, and now the machine wasn't working at all.

'What make of washer is it?' I asked him.

'It's a Hotpoint.'

I whistled.

'One of the old WD 420 models, is it?'

'I don't know. Why?'

'They're feckers for their wobbly transmissions.'

'The point is my machine had a slight leak, and your guy was supposed to fix it, not ruin the damn thing altogether.'

My mobile phone rang. Angela Tenant. I pushed the red button, and set the phone to vibrate.

'Well, if it was leaking the transmission on it was probably already banjaxed,' I said. 'It was only a matter of time.'

'So when is he going to come back and get it working?'

The phone buzzed on the counter. I cut her off again and put it on silent.

'To be honest, it's usually not worth your while. It's hard to get replacement systems, and even when you can, they're very expensive.'

'So what am I supposed to do?'

Then the shop phone rang.

'One minute,' I said. 'O'Brien's Electrical.'

'Kevin?'

Angela's voice. I slammed down the phone. Then I picked up the receiver and left it on the counter.

'Another satisfied customer?'

'No.'

'Well?'

'Well what?'

'My fucking washing machine.'

'I'm afraid you're probably better off getting a new one, at this point.'

He accused me of deliberately breaking his washer so I could flog him a new model, even though we don't sell washing machines. He called me a fucking prick and nearly cracked the glass in the door when he slammed it on the way out.

I didn't have time to worry about what Angela wanted. I was still trying to finish off the books from the previous week, and I had to put in new orders to five different suppliers, and I had two other customers in complaining about Andy. It had been lashing all day, and everyone who came through the door was very wet, and very angry.

At ten past six I checked my phone and I had eleven missed calls. Two more from Angela, three from Mick, and six from Edel.

Why was Edel ringing me?

What had Angela said to her?

I stood looking at my phone for a few minutes. I went and locked the shop door, then came back around behind the counter and looked at my phone again.

I dialled 171 for my voicemail, then cut off the call.

I dialled again. I had five new voice messages.

First message was from Mick, telling me the phone was off the hook.

Second message was from Mick telling me to put the fucking phone back on the hook.

Third message was from Edel. The sound of her voice had never before induced such a powerful urge to vomit.

'Why aren't you answering your phone?' she said. 'The house is flooding.'

Traffic cones barred the turn-off to the cul-de-sac, and I had to drive three hundred yards down the North Strand before I could find somewhere to leave the car. The drains were blocked and the road was mapped by broad, slow streams, rushing creeks and little whirlpools. I pulled my coat over my head and ran back up the street, trying to hop over the puddles and currents and landing my right shoe in the deepest of them.

Turning onto St. Brigid's Avenue was like walking into the News. All the front doors on both sides of the street were wide open and men and women and children carried pots and buckets and bins of water out of their houses and spilled them into the road. Others packed together under umbrellas and shivered and chatted in hushed voices.

'A month's worth of rain in the space of an hour.'

'The wettest day in Dublin since records began.'

'Still no sign of the Council, the useless shower of cunts.'

At the bottom of the road the four girls were stood trembling in their doorway.

'Jesus, girls,' I said.

Angela was struggling to light a damp cigarette with wet fingers and hardly looked at me.

'Edel's inside,' said Katie.

'How would you gauge her mood?' I asked them. They just gaped at me.

There is a small step down into the house from the street, and the hall was under four inches of water, enough to cover the laces of my shoes. Halfway along the hall there are three more stairs down to the back end of the house. The water was a dull green brown colour, and it was cold. It felt like stepping down into a plunge pool. I heard Edel sloshing around in the living room, and braced myself for a bollocking.

She turned to face me as I waded through the door, floorboards floating around her knees.

'Thank God,' she said. 'At last. Can you give me a hand with the couch?'

She was wearing one of my old rain coats, the sleeves rolled up over her elbows, the bottom of it dragging along the surface of the water. The telly and DVD player were on top of the sideboard, and books and DVDs were stacked on the kitchen counter. She had left the table clear, and we lifted the couch up onto it.

'It's probably ruined already,' she said.

'Sorry I took so long,' I said. 'I don't know what's going on with my phone.'

She nodded.

'It started coming up through the floor at five o'clock,' she said. 'The water's still rising. High tide is at twenty past ten, so hopefully it will start to go down then.'

I looked around. The wooden floors and the carpets in the downstairs bedrooms were destroyed. The lower kitchen presses and drawers would all have to be replaced, all the walls would need repainting. The wiring in the sockets would rust, and all the skirting would have to be redone.

'The girls will have to find somewhere else,' said Edel.

I hadn't even thought of that.

'What are you *smiling* at?'

I shook my head and helped her lift the armchairs up onto the couch.

At half ten the flood level did stop rising. By then the girls had packed themselves off to their friends' places, and we locked up the house and headed back to the car. The rain had stopped, and the air felt empty and huge.

We drove in silence for a while, then I turned on the radio. The news was full of reports of flooding from all across the city. I switched the stereo to CD and 'Things Can Only Get Better' came on loud through the speakers.

Halfway through the first chorus, Edel reached down and turned it off.

We featured a story from Matthew Licht in our first anthology,
Various Authors, *and I'm very pleased to have him back. For
more by Matthew, see the above-mentioned story, then his two
anthologies with Salt Publishing:* The Moose Show *is out now,
and* Justine, Joe and the Zen Garbageman *is coming soon.*

Across the Kinderhook

Matthew Licht

Jilly and I were headed upstate to spend a weekend with my old
friend Paul and his family. I hadn't seen Paul for years when he
called to say he'd transferred to his law firm's branch office in
Albany and we were invited. Ordinarily, I welcome any chance to
get out of the city. Maybe the family part gave me the twinge.

The further we got from the sprawling industrial wasteland, the
more I felt like saying I forgot to turn off the stove. But Jilly was
devouring increasingly bucolic autumn scenery through indecently
clean rental car windows. Paul had mentioned something about a
National Park not far from his spread, and I could almost mind-
read her plans to nature-walk, bird-watch and jump on leaf piles
with Paul's kids. Jilly doesn't get as much exposure to trees or kids
as she might like.

We split the main road as soon as possible. When we were
good and lost, I asked Jilly to fish Paul's dictated directions from

my jacket on the back seat and read them aloud as we went along. We reached Paul's place towards dark. The house was pleasantly aglow.

Tousled juvenile delinquents shadowed the windows beside the front door, goggled as strangers emerged from the cheap ticking rental car now parked beside the resident English jeep and German sedan. The taller boy turned to silently yell that the expected guests had arrived, then they both came outside.

Jilly's good with kids. She pinched cheeks, poked bellies, felt biceps and got names. Paul appeared at the door of his home and stood with his hands on the hardwood posts, arms spread in welcoming embrace. He didn't offer to carry bags.

He'd put on a few pounds. He wore a tweedy cardigan. All he needed to be Mr Proud American Homeowner was a pipe stuck in the corner of his mouth, but I figured his wife Nora would've kiboshed any smoking plans on his part. Paul gave Jilly a long, back-patting hug, then turned to me. The look on his heavier face wasn't what I expected.

Nora came out of the kitchen wiping her hands on her apron, a measured smile on her face.

Paul was talking. Nora was talking. Four grown-ups blabbed at each other as the boys stared. Thomas and William were exceptionally good looking. Polite too, or at least calm and quiet. Tall for their ages, which I calculated from the dates Paul had sent engraved announcements to indicate their presence in the world. But there was a kid missing from the equation. There was supposed to be a little girl, named Sophie. I was about to ask the handsome brothers where their sister was, but stopped myself. What if the youngest child had died? That would explain the lost looks on her parents' faces, and the transfer to Albany.

Paul corralled us into the big square living room and fixed a round of gin and tonics. The furniture was heavy, tasteful in the extreme, comfortable. It was nice to be in a living room that made you feel like a human being. The drinks were nice and strong. Whatever was cooking in the kitchen smelled good. Nora set down her glass, still nearly full, excused herself and went to finish getting dinner ready. The boys discreetly escaped to do homework, or watch TV, or wrestle in the rumpus room. Such big houses usually contain rumpus rooms, as well as dens and foyers. That left me, Paul, and Jilly to drink and look at each other with nothing much to say, for the moment.

To cut the silence, I gushed something along the lines of, 'Whoa, you got it made, Paul. Your house is magnificent, Nora looks great, *you* look great, your boys look like movie stars.' Paul said thanks and shot me a look that put us back in fourth grade again.

Jilly knew a bit about Albany. She got Paul to talk about his new home base, the architecture, sordid Empire State politics, William Kennedy's books, local restaurants and nearby natural attractions.

Nora bustled serving trays through the swinging door between dining room and kitchen, which probably cost my annual salary to purchase and install. Muted porcelain, glass and metal sounds while she fussed over the centrepiece and place-settings. She called us to table by ringing a bell or banging a gong.

Nora was issuing instructions on where we were to sit when the boys, washed, combed and tucked, entered the dining room. Between them was a little blonde girl. Instead of holding her hands, they seemed to be herding her with their bodies.

The little girl was so startlingly pretty, I must've blurted something like, 'Who's this little doll, huh?' I expected her to giggle and blush and turn her face away, or at least smile and act bashful while I slowly found out her name and how old she was and would she give her daddy's old friend Joe a kiss hello. The little doll stared straight ahead. Slowly, dreamily, she hoisted herself onto a chair and sat with her hands in her lap. Paul, Nora, Jilly, and I stared as the brothers squirmed in their seats at her sides. They wanted food. They wanted the uneasiness to end.

'This is Sophie, Joe. She is seven years old. She is... she has a *condition*, which we haven't been able to fully understand yet.'

Nora started serving the elaborate dinner. She passed plates and asked how I was doing, if I'd found a publisher or an agent yet. I told her the answer, which she knew already, and said the art-moving company I worked for wasn't doing too badly. Jilly said a friend of ours in LA had plans to turn a story I sent him into the screenplay for his next movie.

Paul's face brightened. 'Hey, that's great, buddy. So you're going to move out west and go totally Hollywood, right?'

The budgets for our friend's movies, I said, usually run in the low four figures.

Paul had done some lawyering for Chicago's Public TV station. There were plenty of creative outlets available, he said, for people like me.

Nora said she was happy with her new teaching post and the quality of the students at SUNY Albany. She was sure her private practice would take off again too, once she found a suitable suite of offices. Paul and Nora were fascinated that Jilly actually made a living as a hand and foot model.

'I had no idea there *was* such a job,' Nora said. She gave Jilly's hands a searching sidelong glance as they moved knife and fork.

'The capon's delicious,' I said. 'And I haven't eaten salsify since I don't know when.'

Nora had no use for sincere compliments at that moment. She was looking at her daughter. The gorgeous little girl had moved.

Slowly, silently, Sophie got down from her chair and walked towards Jilly, and without a word, face turned slightly away, climbed into her lap. Jilly moved back from the table, scraped her chair on the pickled-oak floor. Sophie leaned her head against Jilly's chest and was still. Jilly said, 'Hello, sweetie.'

Moved by the homey scene, I was about to further compliment my hostess on her children. Nora's chin shook. She dropped her fork, pushed her chair away and stumbled towards the kitchen with a hand to her face. Paul seemed thunderstruck. 'She's never done anything like that before.'

Nora regained mastery over her emotions, came back from the kitchen with a casserole of curried pumpkin and yams. We passed our plates to receive. Sophie let Jilly feed her a few forkfuls.

'Amazing,' Paul whispered, as though afraid to startle a wild animal or break a magic spell. 'The doctors said this might never happen.' He reached for his wife's hand, squeezed it.

Jilly wiped the little girl's mouth. 'Good stuff, huh?'

Sophie nodded, without moving her eyes. Tears rolled down Nora's cheeks.

'Jilly's just naturally great with children,' I said.

'You don't understand,' Nora said.

Sophie didn't get down from Jilly's lap until Nora brought out a second pot of coffee. The boys asked to be excused. The little girl followed her brothers into the TV room like a ghost.

'She seems to enjoy certain programmes,' Paul said. 'Especially nature shows, underwater documentaries, African wildlife, Arctic landscapes. Other things set her off. Certain sounds, or being buckled into her seat in the car... it's unpredictable. She becomes enraged.' He made fists, shook them. 'We have to watch her, then. She bangs her head and scratches herself. But most of the time, there's nothing. A wall.'

The air had cleared. We headed back into the living room and sat talking about exotic psychiatric disorders and their effects on parents, siblings and other children, doctors' impotence, drastic measures used to spark awareness, special schools, hopelessness countered by uncertainty.

'Some children like Sophie have breakthroughs. I mean, it's not as though they suddenly, overnight, become fully responsive, interactive, so-called *normal*, but there are documented cases of children like Sophie who are able to attend school, find jobs, who can even travel on their own and have relationships.'

Paul went around with mouldy-label, dusty-bottle port from his collection. Tasty, but Nora didn't want any.

'You might be a door that's opened for our child,' she said to Jilly. 'She responded when you spoke to her. She was listening to you. You know, she's never let me pick her up. Even in the first few months, she wanted to nurse without being held. She'd scream, shake and go full-on paralyzed if I so much as touched her. She'd pull her head away from my breast.'

Nora could probably have used a shot of port.

'Same with me,' Paul said. 'Or maybe even worse. I mean, she allowed me even *less* contact. She only let us dress her until she could do it on her own. Takes her forever, but that's the way it has to be. She lets her brothers lead her around, but she won't hold their hands. She'll sit in a stroller, but you can't strap her in. She likes being pushed, though. She enjoys speed, in general.'

'It's painful, terribly,' Nora said, still caught up in her story, not listening to Paul's part. 'Imagine, your own infant refuses you. She refused everything except what she needed to live. Painful.'

'We go to therapy one night a week. Each. Separately. We've decided to leave the boys out of counselling, for now. They're coping with the situation pretty well. They have each other. They don't talk about what's wrong with their sister, not yet.'

'Sophie's never said a word. Sometimes I think she hears what we're saying, that she's taking in our voices, our language, that something, at least, is registering. Other times, I'm not sure. I get the feeling there's nothing there, or whatever ought to be there comes and goes whenever it wants to.'

Jilly looked at the clock on the mantelpiece and said, 'Maybe she'll let me put her to bed. I could read her a story or something.'

'Oh by all means,' Paul said. 'Please, please try.'

Jilly got up and went to the room where the children were. Nora followed her, to watch.

'Sometimes she lets her brothers lead her upstairs,' Paul said. 'Usually she just falls asleep wherever she happens to be. We can carry her, then. We can hold her and talk to her when she's asleep.'

Nora came back into the living room shaking her head. She went to the cherry-wood Biedermeier console where Paul kept the booze and poured herself a healthy shot of something peach-coloured.

'I can't believe this,' she said, when she sat back down. 'It's like I wasn't there, I was invisible to my own baby. I felt like I should leave the two of them alone. But she's my baby, my daughter. I should be overjoyed, Paul. I know I should. This might be what we've been hoping for, but instead I feel angry.'

'Nora, we have to control our feelings.'

I tried to become invisible. Husband-and-wife, family-therapy talk was on the way. I whispered about fresh air and went outside.

Leaves covered the lawn in front of the house. Paul wasn't big on raking them, or didn't have time, or hired someone to take care of property chores once a week or so. I wandered, tried not to make noise. Through the windows into the living room, I saw Paul put his arm around Nora on their gigantic red velvet couch. They were talking about the strange thing that had happened.

Upstairs and to the right, in a bedroom, my long-suffering love Jilly was getting to know a little girl who until a short while ago had refused to let herself be known at even the most primitive level by those inextricably linked to her. Whatever was wrong with the little girl, Sophie, wasn't my business or my problem. Jilly was a different matter. We'd been together over fifteen years at that point.

We'd been living together a year when we had what relationship counsellors might call a meaningful discussion about children. I didn't want any. Maybe if I'd had some success in life and work, or thought I was something worth reproducing, I would've felt differently. I told Jilly I loved her, but if she needed children to be happy, she'd better leave. She stayed.

The light from Sophie's room glowed ominously. I couldn't see into that window, no matter how I shifted around in the scenery. Paul's property included venerable trees, but getting a perch on even the lowest branches involved the risk of a neck-breaking fall. I wanted to see if Jilly and Sophie were bonding the way women and girls do, or if there was something else involved.

Nora suspected that her daughter took in information, but giving info back and adding to it is a different story. Human communication requires practice, trial and error. Nobody listens to a piece of music and suddenly bursts into virtuoso piano or guitar. Or maybe some lucky people can. I'm not one of them. I didn't know if it was possible for a child who'd been mute her whole seven-year-old life to suddenly start talking. Maybe it was just a matter of meeting somebody she felt like talking to.

When I started shivering, I went back inside. Paul and I talked about what had happened to people we knew in school. Nora sat in silence. She refilled her glass and became practically autistic.

Jilly came downstairs not long after Sophie's brothers turned off the TV and came into the living room to kiss their parents goodnight. They shook hands with me, the stranger to whom they might have been ordered to be polite and thus cause to feel welcome. The way they held themselves and stuck together in a weird situation that was no fault of theirs was impressive. Jilly entered, was stared at, sat next to me. She looked at us looking at her and said, 'What a beautiful little girl you have.'

Which was like saying the sky is blue, the ocean deep. Not what the beautiful little girl's anxious parents wanted to hear.

Nora almost shrieked. 'What happened?'

Jilly was taken aback. A mother's hysteria about her child's welfare was something new. Most of our friends are child-free couples like ourselves.

'Oh, nothing,' Jilly said. 'I put her on the bed and we sat there and just sort of looked each other over...'

Tears flowed down the tearbeds on Nora cheeks.

'... then I, you know, started getting her ready for bed. I found a T-shirt in a drawer, figured she'd be warm enough... I mean, it's so nice and cosy in here. Then I told her a story my mother used to tell me when I was around her age...'

Paul leaned forward in his armchair. 'Jilly, please, this is extremely important: did Sophie say anything? Did she give any sign she knows what's going on, that she knows who she is, who we are? Or that she *wants* to know?'

'What did you do?' Nora said. 'What did you *do*? Tell me. I need to know. Why won't my own baby look at me? Why won't she let me pick her up?'

It's rough, hearing a woman talk the way Nora was talking, being more or less forced to watch a woman show herself more than naked. Not all fun and games, being a woman, a mother.

Jilly was on the spot, and she doesn't like it. 'She didn't say anything. She didn't really *do* anything. But she was listening to me. She seemed happy.'

Jilly meant to say something nice, something kind, I think, but it sent Nora into another fit of anguish. Paul gathered his wife together, said good night and told us to help ourselves to anything we wanted or needed.

Upstairs, in the bedroom Nora had assigned us even though we didn't have a marriage license, I stared while Jilly got undressed. That wasn't just any old Shetland sweater she pulled over her head. Neither was that an ordinary T-shirt. Those were no run-through-the-mill Lee's jeans she pulled down and off her legs.

'You going to sleep in your clothes? You going to gawk at me all night long?'

'Better get used to it, lover. If you're going to go around resurrecting the blind and multiplying loaves into fishes.'

'Stop it. I feel horrible.'

'What? Why? It was fantastic. That weird kid came alive. You were a shining light.'

'But I didn't do anything. It just happened. Put yourself in that poor woman's place.'

'Nora? She's way too uptight. Don't worry. You've given her hope.'

She shook out her hair. 'You don't understand much about women.'

'Guess not.'

Jilly reached over me to turn out the bedside lamp. The image of a child's bedroom, seen from the darkness outside, came on in my head when the room went black. The disturbing picture wouldn't vanish. Something had happened between Jilly and the beautiful, strange little girl. Still dressed, lying atop a quilt, blankets and sheets, I whispered, 'She said something, didn't she? She spoke to you.'

'Who, Sophie?'

'Tell me what she said.'

There was a long pause. 'I don't think I should tell you, Joe.'

'If the world's coming to an end or Jesus is coming back or the sky's falling, I want to know.'

'We shouldn't have done what we did, that time.'

The way she said it made me want to tell her stop, I didn't really want to know after all. But I couldn't help saying, 'What're you talking about? When?'

'When I got pregnant that time.'

'But we talked it over. It wasn't just me. We agreed the timing was bad and we didn't want to keep it.'

'It would've been a girl, Joe. I got the nurse to tell me. Usually they won't tell you anything, even if you ask. Or that's what the nurse said. But I got her to tell me anyway.'

That was definitely something I didn't want to know. I felt sick. Let's face it, I talked Jilly into having the procedure done, maybe even bullied her. I didn't want to have a kid.

'Wait a minute, baby. Their little girl told you we shouldn't have had an abortion? She's seven years old.'

'You got it wrong. She said it was okay. She touched my face while I was telling her the story of a girl who talks to strangers, and said it was all right. And I knew that's what she was talking about. But even though she was telling me it was all right and not to worry, I knew I shouldn't have done it.'

'We did it together, Jilly. We're in this together, whatever happens. Forever.'

She said sure and turned over. Her breathing soon became deep and regular. She was asleep. Not me. Couldn't even close my eyes. I went downstairs to the living room and tried to read the book I'd brought with me, but it didn't help. Neither did watching TV at minimum volume, with the door closed, in Paul's well-equipped media centre. I borrowed one of the jackets hung on hooks by the door and went outside.

A river ran near Paul's house. I followed the water sound, scrambled through underbrush and walked along boulder-strewn banks in the half-moon light. Hard going, in city shoes, but I pushed on, hoped a ghost or some other monster of the dark would shove me into the river so I could drown. I was crying for the first time since the last blow-up with my old man, but at least that was something that'd never happen again in this life. Maybe my old man was right about being alive, about being a man, about everything I told him he'd got wrong because he was brainwashed by society-at-large. Now I couldn't ask him about anything, unless I wanted to howl at the moon. I couldn't talk to him, or to that other little girl, the one I never saw or spoke to, even though she was mine and part of me. I'd never see her, or hear her talk, hadn't allowed it. I saw Sophie, So-*fie*-uh, daughter of an old friend I no longer knew and didn't particularly like any more. Saw her beautiful face turned away, empty of emotion or recognition, as far as I was concerned, in any case. Jilly was a different world, for the otherwise aloof little girl, and for me.

The river kept running. There were no ghosts around. I wanted to jump in, so the river could wash my mind clean or wash it clean away when my head hit rocks under the swirling current.

I got back to the house towards cold hazy late-autumn dawn. The door was closed but not locked. I went in, dirty, wet, scraped, gouged, bleeding and half frozen. Paul was already up, already on the phone, leaving frantic, confused messages on answering machines in various doctors' and psychiatrists' offices. He wanted professional advice on how to follow up on the unexpected event of the evening before. He barely noticed me.

Nora stared at her gleaming, laser-guided coffee machine. She scoped me wearing her husband's jacket covered in burdocks, decaying leaves and mud, but said nothing. I went upstairs.

Jilly was still asleep. I shut the door quietly and went down the hall.

Sophie was sleeping too. Her eyes moved, her hands twitched. Asleep, she looked the same as children who have nothing wrong with them. I tried to picture what sort of dreams a child like her might dream. I couldn't make a sound, didn't want to awaken that displaced angel and frighten her. Instead, I woke up and frightened Jilly. I grabbed her like I was drowning, like I'd just heard the bomb go off, the one that means it's all over, for all of us.

She choked out a scream, tried to hit me in the head, then realized it was just her usual boyfriend, looking wild. I squeezed her and said I'm sorry over and over. I wouldn't let her go. She let me hold her hand while she peed and then brushed her teeth. She let me get in the shower with her.

Nora was making Belgian waffles with another sparkling kitchen gadget while Paul frothed milk, whipped cream and chopped strawberries. Their children were watching an educational Saturday morning TV show. Tension fell when Jilly and I entered the kitchen and adjacent breakfast nook. Enquiries were made as to sleep quality. No one asked what I'd been up to during the night.

Nora, her cool, collected self again, called the children to come eat. If she'd told me go comb your hair and shave or else no coffee and waffles, I'd have gone without a peep. The boys looked lordly in pyjamas and robes. The little girl was in the T-shirt Jilly had put on her. She must've laboriously put on her pink romper pants and powder-blue terry cloth slippers by herself. Everyone stared at Sophie and Jilly. Paul and Nora were probably wondering whether it'd be worse if the miracle were repeated, or not.

Sophie sat and absently watched her brother cut up her fluffy, steaming waffle topped with a cloud of sweet cream, local farm-bought maple syrup and fruit flown in from Guatemala. After the rest of us were nearly done eating, she tucked in slowly, holding her fork as close to the end of its handle as possible, pinky raised. Everyone except Jilly stared to see if she'd do something, show a spark. Then we spoke as though nothing were the matter, sneaking glances. Mysterious disorders of affect might be deepened by this sort of morbid attention, extreme self-consciousness made progressively worse.

Jilly asked, 'Sophie, would you pass the syrup?'

Dead silence hung in the air. The younger boy, William, started to do it instead, but Sophie put down her fork and slowly picked up the beige plastic jug in both hands and carried it around the table like an important gift.

'Thanks, sweetie. Here, do you want to finish my strawberries and cream? Too much for me.'

Sophie looked at Jilly. Her eyebrows moved a shade closer together, her eyes shone for a moment. How I wish I could sit in your lap, nice lady. I wish I could let you feed me strawberries while you hold me tight, but I cannot. Forces beyond my control and understanding prevent me.

Sophie went back to her place and resumed eating, slowly, as though she couldn't taste the food, which was nothing but fuel to keep the body alive.

Nora wiped her mouth. 'Sophie? Darling? Will you bring Mommy the syrup too, please?'

Sophie's fork cut through waffle and clicked on her plate. Another pastry square rose mouthward and disappeared. The syrup stayed where it was. Before the scene became unbearable, Thomas, the older boy, grabbed the plastic bottle's quaint round finger-hole and brought it to his mother. She seized him in a bear hug and cried into his hair, rocked him and said thank you darling over and over.

After that thoroughly uncomfortable breakfast, Jilly got the boys to show her their favourite spots along the river and in the forest, where, she told me later, they tried Indian-style spear fishing and built a fort.

Paul took me in his racing-green jeep to inspect a piece of property he planned to acquire to prevent it from ever being commercially developed, unless he decided to sell. Nora took her daughter in the other car to be inspected by neurologists, psychiatrists and psychologists. She wanted to tell them what happened and demand explanations.

Paul and I roamed his future acres. He pointed out trees and shrubs and said their names for the city boy. Under a copper beech, he put a hand on my shoulder and solemnly said, 'You and Jilly have got to stay with us, Joe. Please. At least for a while. I think this is the breakthrough we've been hoping for. Please.'

'Listen, Paul... we'd love to help. Jilly would, I mean. But I've got jobs coming up and I'm in the middle of something else, too. This was supposed to be just a weekend getaway... Jilly's got bookings next week. I don't think we can do it.'

'We could work out financial arrangements. That's not a problem. Joe, I'm begging you.'

'It's not up to me, Paul. Ask Jilly. I mean, she's the one who, well, you know.'

Jilly said she couldn't back out of her engagements.

Since nothing happened the next day, Sunday — no communication of any kind with Sophie, that is — Jilly said she thought it might be better if some time passed before they saw each other again. The specialists Nora immediately consulted were unable to affirm or contradict Jilly's theory, or offer other suggestions. So we said we'd come up again the next weekend perhaps, or the one after that.

Last time we went up, when they were in the upstairs bedroom together, Sophie called Jilly Mama. Tell me the story again, Mama. Jilly didn't tell Sophie's parents what she'd said. No point causing Nora further anguish. She told me instead. So I went out for another night-time walk by the river. After a mile or so, I stopped and sat on a dry boulder and looked at another, smaller rock under the rippling water. The white rock shone like another reflection of the moon. Maybe it was marble, or quartz.

In uncertain times, we tend towards nostalgia. We watch Downton Abbey, drink ginger beer, and play traditional boardgames made in China with real wooden pieces. In the small town where I live, many household goods are more readily available as antiques than as new products. Enter Die Booth, with a story about our relationship with the objects of the past.

Phantoms

Die Booth

The scariest thing I've ever seen was my granddad's phantom.

My granddad, his name was Roger and he collected weird stuff. He ran a junk shop — that is, an *Emporium of Curious Vintage Ephemera*. It was still a junk shop. Sometimes he got hold of something that was worth something for cheap, then that would get sold straight away to a proper antiques place. Just because he sold tat, didn't mean he didn't know his stuff. Granddad just liked tat, said the things people threw out were more interesting. His main profits didn't come from the good stuff, either: they came from the rubbish. People love to sift through piles of interesting old crap, the detritus of past lives, in the hope of finding a treasure, and sometimes Granddad hid one in there for them to find, too. His job; it was his hobby.

Most times the stock came in lots from attic sales and house clearances, and if there was anything really interesting in there, Granddad would winkle it out and keep it for his own private hoard. His collection, he called it. He liked medical stuff; the plate runners in the rooms above the shop were all lined up with little old glass bottles of green and jewel blue, 'not to be taken' embossed on their faceted sides. These were dug up in their hundreds from Edwardian rubbish tip sites by enthusiastic prospectors, although you see them less and less now. There was a cabinet, with metal slide plates still housing faded paper labels, full of Victorian prosthetic eyes propped in eggcups and saucers like exotic glazed sweets. There were shallow porcelain toothpaste tubs with beautiful scrolled lettering on the lids. There was other stuff, too: old tailcoats with disintegrating quilted silk linings, stacks upon stacks of brittle vinyl 78s, rust-pocked biscuit tins full of a wealth of mismatched buttons and mystery keys. A giant yellow tea cup from a long-ago fairground ride. And there was the lay figure.

The lay figure came from a broken-up country estate called Hepcote Manor. It always made me sad to hear about estates being broken up; I pictured men with crowbars prising apart the very walls of big, old houses. I suppose I wasn't too far off the mark. It still astounds me what you can buy for money and it was even more bizarre back then before vintage became really fashionable. The items that were processed through Granddad's shop commanded me: church confessionals and tapestries streaked black with damp, fragments of stained glass and original Tudor oak panelling, swathes of hand-painted wallpaper with the crust of paste still dried on the back. Headstones. Watch chains made of woven hair.

I always thought the lay figure was rude. There was something dark about the name, although Granddad explained that 'lay' was the same as lay preachers in a church and that the figure was used by well-to-do artists in place of a human model. If someone's daughter didn't want to sit draped in grapevines or whatever for hours on end, she'd pose for the initial sketch and then the lay figure would take her place; dressed in her costume, correct to the inch, smiling her placid smile. When she came to us there was white powder in the lay figure's blonde chignon where the artist had made her up to look like an older sitter.

The lay figure was naked. I think this was what disturbed me so much about her. She was not only naked but perfect, in a floss-haired, tiny-waisted, dispassionate kind of way. Inside her stitched padded cotton, behind her painted, gesso-covered face was an armature. She was jointed in the same way as a human being: she could hold any pose with docile ease. I found myself thinking of her metal skeleton lurking beneath the padding much more often than I thought with horror about real skeletons of bone and gristle. Granddad loved her. He referred to Hepcote as 'Hepcat manner' and named her Tallulah Blue, which he thought was a good beatnik name. She sat demurely cross-legged on a ladder-back chair behind the counter, wearing only a black beret, a celluloid cigarillo holder between her elegant fingers, smiling, smiling...

That little half-smile was infuriating. Her mute acceptance somehow made the fact that she didn't have any clothes on even more indecent. I started taking clothes from the lots that came into the shop and dressing her up, because her nudity made me feel embarrassed in a way that I couldn't quite put into words, not even to Granddad. Granddad thought it was cute. I think he thought I saw her as just a giant fashion doll, which I suppose she was, in a way. As soon as she was clothed, I liked her a lot more. I even started to talk to her sometimes, although I still found myself watching her out of the corner of my eye when I was alone in the shop. I couldn't help myself.

I was never cool at school. I was a swot and I was posh, so it was judged. I sat on my own, absorbed with drawing elaborate networks of glass pipes in fantastic mad science laboratories, each beaker filled with a different bubbling, fluorescent elixir. I wasn't scared of anything. Granddad's shop made the unknown something to be explored and befriended. These days I'd probably be given special treatment and a day pass to the school counsellor. Back then, in church school, I was tolerated with disdain.

There was this girl called Beth and she bullied me for five years. Looking back, I'm not entirely sure how this worked, because she was nearly as unpopular as I was. She was tall for a twelve-year-old and massively overweight; she was spoiled and overconfident and she hated me. She did this thing which drove me crazy, which was that she copied me. Whenever I came to school with a new pair of blue ribbons at the end of my plaits, the next day Beth would have some too — wider, bluer, shinier and obviously more expensive — tied into her thick, yellow hair. When I was bought a new pencil tin at the start of term, Beth turned up with the same one, filled with twice as many miniature pencils and double the amount of rubbers shaped like pink love-hearts and ladybirds. My mum didn't take Beth seriously. I suppose it was a deviously subtle form of torture, even for a girl. Mum said that 'imitation is the sincerest form of flattery,' and told me that Beth was jealous. How come Beth was so jealous, I wondered, when she always had better stuff than me?

Granddad just said, 'Let's see her copy this,' and pinned a World War Two air-force sweetheart brooch to my blazer lapel.

Beth loved babies. She was going to be a midwife when she grew up. I wonder if she ever made it. Personally, I didn't see the appeal: I wanted to be Alice in Wonderland, or Mary Poppins, or a scientist.

'Girls can't be scientists,' Beth would sneer, with the certainty of one never lightly contradicted. They had a name for me at school; Beth thought of it. They called me Slim. They only called me that because it rhymes with Pym, which is my surname. Looking back, it's even kind of flattering that they couldn't find anything more about me to ridicule with a nickname, but at the time they had this way of saying it, Slim Pym, this jeering, monotonous way of saying it that made me feel physically sick. I tried to brush it off. I even tried to adopt it for my own — Slim, my nickname, like some super-chic 1930s gangster's moll — but it didn't work. It wasn't the word; it was the intention with which it was spoken.

I always thought that Beth was a fat name, just the sound of it: plosive and pillowy like a puffball fungus exploding. Poisonous. Poisonous girl.

Then one day the phantom arrived.

It was an unseasonably colourless day in late August. The air hung miserably cool, and mean clouds bleached the sky white. An antique shop in Caergwrly was closing down and bargaining off un-saleable stock, and I'd never seen Granddad so excited. I wasn't really sure what the occasion was but his high spirits were infectious and made the blank day feel like Christmas Eve. It was like Granddad was another kid my age, only better because he knew stuff and had money and grownups listened to him.

'Anna, you have to help me choose what to have,' Granddad said, lifting me onto the overstuffed leather seat of a vintage dentists chair like the cockpit of a steampunk spaceship. I adjusted the wing mirrors and tried to work the tip-back mechanism. I loved going to the dentists. I had perfect teeth. Granddad passed me a disenfranchised bureau drawer; it too was full of perfect teeth, porcelain dentures and single crowns, more beautiful than ropes of pearls. I began to sort out my favourites. That place, that day, was better than fairyland.

So I walked into the front of the shop with a careful armful of delicate blown-glass distilling equipment, my pockets clicking with porcelain incisors, to find Granddad in intense discussion with the shopkeeper. Something was laid on the countertop between them. It was level with my face. It was white and long and looked like a doll.

'Let me see,' I said, nudging in beneath Granddad's arm. It was weird how he showed me that thing. How he started to explain its use, too quickly, as if somehow he instinctively knew that out of the catalogue of oddities I'd been introduced to over the years this would be the one to instil instant, frigid dread inside me. Maybe it was a little to do with how he acted that made me so nervous. How he held off from using the term 'phantom' for so long, like it was a dangerous prediction and not just a technical term.

'In the olden days they'd use these to train ladies who'd deliver babies, to give them some practice. Sort of like those kiss of life dummies they have at St John's Ambulance. It's like a baby doll, to get them used to how a baby being born would feel.'

'Midwives,' I said flatly, eyeing the phantom. It was the same shape as a baby and the same size and weight, and it was made of some of the same stuff babies are made of, too. The phantom was lank and limp as a hatched chick, made of butter-soft white kid leather stretched over the brittle skeleton of a human foetus. Its bulbous eye sockets were tight and blind. It was at once real and not real. It was the most terrible thing I'd ever looked upon but I couldn't take my eyes off it. I think Granddad knew because I'd gone quiet.

'I just wanted to have a look, Anna. I'd never seen one before. We don't have to buy it.'

'No,' I said, 'We have to buy him.'

I knew that babies crawled, but when I dreamed of the phantom he'd be tottering along upright on his fragile, mummified legs, the arid bubble of his skull wobbling like a poppy head on the thin, dry stalk of his neck. He smelled of old, of a barely perceptible amalgamation of all the dusty stuff in Granddad's shop: wood, leather, polish. Like the inside of the glass-eye cabinet. I'd carry the phantom around the shop, the sight and feel of the twiggy bones just beneath the skin making my scalp crawl. I wouldn't let him out of my sight, in that way an arachnophobe will intently watch a spider, because as soon as you turn away you're not quite sure where it is anymore. You carry your fear around with you; you live with it day to day. Maybe your fear becomes familiar and a little less scary, but likewise you never rest from it for a second.

I remember the day I turned the tables on Beth very well.

Beth was sitting at a canteen table, doggedly spooning apple pie and custard into her mouth. Her arm moved in a cyclical motion. Her jaw worked like a cow chewing the cud. She looked like a cartoon. The custard, I can remember, was very yellow like buttercups, with a rubbery skin that formed repeatedly on the surface as it cooled. Lily-liver yellow with a thick skin. When I walked past with my green plastic lunch tray held out like a shield, Beth swivelled her eyes towards me. She said:

'Your granddad steals stuff from the tip to sell and Lauren says all you ever eat at your house is spaghetti hoops.'

I could see inside her mouth, full of chewed-up pie. I replied:

'When you're a midwife, you have to birth dead babies.'

I don't know where it came from, it just popped into my head and I said it. Beth paused for a moment too long, weighing me up, before she said disdainfully:

'No you don't.'

But that fraction of hesitation was enough to show me the way. An edge. A chink.

'You do. My granddad's got one in his shop. If you don't shut up about him, I'll make it come and *get you.*'

'No he hasn't. You're a liar,' Beth said. Her eyes narrowed. 'You're abnormal, Slim Pym.'

For some reason, the name didn't grate as much as usual. I had her on the run. I said, 'Dead babies,' and Beth pushed her tray away and walked off.

I should have left it there. I suppose what I did in the next few days was bullying too, but even now I feel like the little cow deserved it. Every time I caught her eye I smiled, smiled, and she looked unsure.

On Thursday nights Dad played snooker at the club and when Mum went with him I stayed at Granddad's. We'd sit on the sofa and eat ice lollies half-red, half-orange, the kind made entirely of additives with congealed syrup gumming up the sticks. We'd watch dated sitcoms about the war or trains and I was allowed up until nine o'clock when Granddad would switch off the spare bedroom light for me and gently close the door.

I'd never stayed up so late before; it was such an effort not to give in to sleep. I didn't like the spare room with no lights on, so I stayed under the bed covers and held my watch right up to my face to check the time by its little luminous hands.

A quarter to midnight. I crept out of bed, padded downstairs in my socks. The grey night-time light made everything look two dimensional, unreal. The wooden banister felt cold beneath my palm: I hadn't noticed before then how warm the shop usually was in the daytime.

I'd never been into the shop after dark. The half light made the familiar look strange. The glass eyes in their cabinet seemed to gleam with their own illumination; they followed me. I'd forgotten what was stored in corners. Everything looked like it was moving.

I nearly screamed when I saw her sitting there: the sound clogged in my throat, blocked my airways. I'd forgotten about Tallulah and for a moment I thought it was a real person behind the counter. Still in the moonlight, I knew at any moment she might lurch into un-life and lunge for me, her steel bones squeezing me until I popped: in the dark, Tallulah had stopped being my friend.

The phantom wasn't on display. When he was stored away, he lived in a box beneath the counter, wrapped in acid-free tissue paper. I edged past Tallulah, trying not to touch. To touch might activate her. I had to get the counter key from behind the till to unlock the sliding cupboard doors; the noise of the key twisting in the lock seemed loud enough to bring police sirens squealing. It wasn't really loud, though. I slid the doors back. I reached over a stack of slipware plates to lift out the phantom's box. Folding back the tissue paper, I thought what an awful, mummified little thing it was. I bunched the tissue back in place, trying to make it look like there was still something in the box. Stowing it back on the shelf, I even remembered to lock the cupboard door again — Tallulah's painted blue eyes scrutinising my back — before I escaped back upstairs to the dubious safety of the spare room.

That night, I dreamt I was in a maze, pursued by the stop-motion Minotaur from 'Sinbad and the Eye of the Tiger'. I couldn't see it, but it was there just outside of my field of view; the sound of screeching metal on metal encroaching. I ran and ran but I couldn't find my way out. I finally came to the centre of the maze, where the phantom stretched out its arms towards me, crying: monsters before and behind.

Beth was in the corner of the playground furthest from the school doors. She was swinging a skipping rope round like a majorette's ribbon, surrounded by her followers. I'd been hoping she'd approach me, say something mean, give me a reason; but for once she left me alone. I walked over. She looked at me with a mixture of contempt and wariness. The skipping rope swished a serpentine wave on the tarmac.

'Get lost, Slim Pym. You smell of the dump.'

Someone laughed. Someone repeated 'dump'.

'I've got something to show you,' I said.

From under my jumper I took a plastic carrier bag and unrolled it. There was something heavy in the bottom. Beth's eyes narrowed. Reaching in, I drew out the phantom.

In daylight the phantom lost all its magic and was all the more terrible for it. The sum of its parts: dead child, stretched leather, old medicine. The crowd dispersed rapidly, even the curious edging backwards and making dismayed noises. I thrust the phantom towards Beth and she squealed in horror. Her eyes sort of bulged as if she was squeezed around the neck by steel fingers. Then she did something I wasn't expecting. She lashed out with her looped skipping rope, which hooked around the phantom and pulled it from my hands to the floor. Then she ran: the slap of her retreating footsteps, the sound of the centuries-old skull of a stillborn cracking.

I felt sick with guilt as I bent to pick up the phantom. I felt embarrassed, but nobody was looking; they were all too scared to stick around. It didn't feel as much of a triumph as it should have, although at least I never had any more trouble off Beth afterwards. Gingerly testing the phantom's skull, I could feel the two broken parts grate against each other slightly.

I never did tell Granddad. I'm not sure if he ever noticed; if he did, he kept quiet. I took the phantom home again in my school bag, then back to the shop on Saturday. I was going to try and smuggle it back into its box, but instead I sat it propped on the counter. It wasn't scary anymore. I just felt sorry for it, as if I'd hurt it for a really selfish reason. I decided it needed a name, a sort of medal of honour for saving me from Beth, so I called it George after the saint who slew the dragon. That Saturday, Tallulah was wearing an old smocked cotton nightdress almost the same colour as her calico skin, a blue woollen old-lady snood stretched over her blonde hair. I positioned her arms into a rocking shape; the ratchet of her metal joints had somehow lost its awful mystery. I arranged George cradled there, mother and baby, silent and watchful. Tallulah: smiling her enigmatic half-smile, keeping all of our secrets.

We don't often publish stories in the second person, but sometimes that's just the way a story needs to be written. This is also one of those cases where a biographical note on the author can really inform the reading of a story: Luiza Sauma was born in Rio, but grew up in London.

Carolina Carioca

Luiza Sauma

You said you dreamed of angels the night we met and that it was a sign. I didn't believe in such things, but I listened to your story with the sort of politeness I only afford to foreigners. I was the foreigner: an Englishman in Rio de Janeiro. It was a morning like any another, apart from the fact that I had woken up with you in my bed.

'It's a sign,' you said in Portuguese. 'I can feel it.'

In the dream, the tin roof of your mother's house in Favela do Vidigal, at the end of the beach, had blown off, and the angels were shining down on you, smiling in a pleasant white light. You told me there were five of them, neither woman nor man; neither white nor black nor índio, but in between.

You laughed and your brown skin seemed to glow.

It wasn't the kind of thing girls said in London after a one-night stand. That's what I thought it would be, when you came home with me: a one-night stand. I'd been living in Ipanema for over two years: bumming around, teaching English, learning Portuguese and burning my British skin to a deep brown, so that my eyes wrinkled, making me look at least five years older than twenty-five. I was feeling useless and bored, and thinking of going home to start some sort of career. You were nineteen, a born-and-bred Carioca who worked six days a week at a kiosk on Ipanema beach, and went to church on Sundays.

We had met on the beach the day before. A weekday: Monday. I wasn't at work, because really, I didn't work very much. The beach was mostly empty, apart from a few tourists and rich Brazilian slackers with nothing better to do. I was alone, thinking about London, watching the surf. I saw you at your wooden kiosk on the black-and-white pavement by the sand. You were beautiful, but I'd become used to girls like you: dark skinned, firmly curved and long haired. I chose a spot far away from the water, close to you, so I could keep an eye. The slackers kept going up to your kiosk, buying one beer after another. By the end of the day, their faces were pink with alcohol, their faces relaxed with easy living. The sort of kids your mother was paid to raise.

After five o'clock, the sun started going down, the sand went grey-blue in the dusk and the favela at the end of the beach – your favela – began twinkling with multicoloured lights. You and your boss started packing up, then he went home. You stayed, closing up the kiosk. I decided to go over: I wouldn't be seeing girls like you for much longer.

'Hi,' you said, looking up and seeing me.

You smiled, but later I would realise it was a customer-service smile, not a real one.

'Can I buy a beer?' I said in Portuguese.

'We're closed,' you said. '*Desculpe.*'

'How about somewhere else? Can I buy a beer somewhere else?'

'Yes, there are lots of bars around here.'

'I mean for you. Can I buy *you* a beer?'

You laughed, genuinely this time. And then you told me your name: Carolina. We went to a touristy bar on Rua Vinicius de Moraes; a soulless, wood-panelled place, but it was nice sitting outside, feeling the evening breeze. At first, you didn't want to go in there.

'I don't go out in Zona Sul,' you said, wrinkling your nose.

'Where do you go?'

'Up there,' you said, pointing up at the hills.

But we had a good time. We drank beer and ate cheese dough balls. You told me about your family, your mother and your younger sister, who lived together in a two-room house your father built before he passed away.

'Gringos ask me out all the time,' you said. 'I never went out with one before, though.'

'What made you come with me?' I said.

'Don't know,' you said. 'Nothing better to do.'

You laughed; it was a joke. Sweat was running down my back, cooling me down as it trickled.

Before we went to bed, you called your sister to let her know you were staying with a friend. Your mother didn't need to know: she was a maid and slept most nights at her employer's flat, right in front of the beach, two blocks from my flat. The next morning, you told me about your dream and I realised it wasn't a one-night stand.

We saw more of each other. Everything I did, everything I was, seemed exciting to you: my blond hair, my accent, my 'English things'. I visited you at the kiosk, and you stayed over a lot. After two months, you told your mother that you had an English boyfriend. We often spent Sunday afternoons at your house, eating her feijoada. She seemed pleased to have me there, but kept saying, 'Whatever you do, don't take her away from me.' You rolled your eyes.

I took you away. It was April. Rio was sliding from another hot, humid summer into a hot, humid autumn. In London, it was spring. You asked what the weather was like over there. I told you that the sky was always grey, but that it was still the best city in the world.

'Better than Rio?' you said. 'Then why did you come here?'

You had never seen another city, let alone another country. You had never been on a plane. When it started up its violent burring, you grabbed my hand and shrieked, 'Adam, is this normal?'

I laughed and you punched me in the arm.

In London, we rented a cheap ex-council flat in Brockley. The city was, as I had warned you, mostly grey, from the pavements to the sky. But I hadn't told you that once in a while, the sky was as blue as the finest day in Rio, and the sun shone down on the blossomed trees, and everyone spent the day outdoors, looking happy and getting sunburnt. On one of the fine days, I took you on a tour of London on one of those double-decker buses for tourists, with the roof sliced off; even though I had lived in the city nearly all my life, I'd never been on one of those buses, never been to the Tower of London or Buckingham Palace or any of the places you wanted to visit.

In the evenings, there were pubs, restaurants and people's houses. I had to do a tour of duty, meeting up with family and friends. You could speak maybe thirty words of English, but you smiled and nodded at the right times, and everyone thought you were charming and pretty.

'But what do you have in common?' said my friend Kirsty one night at the pub, while you were at the bar and we were outside, smoking cigarettes.

'I love her,' I said, like a schoolboy.

Kirsty laughed and tapped ash onto the ground.

You went to English classes. You met my parents. They were excited to meet you, but disappointed that you couldn't engage in conversation. You kept your eyes low during dinner, looking embarrassed and smiling your customer-service smile when someone caught your eye. After a bit, we almost forgot you were there, and started chatting away in English, about the things I'd seen and my plans in London.

'Do they like me?' you said, in the car on the way back.

I got a job, teaching English at a language school. It paid shit, but it was better than nothing. At first you spent a few days hiding in the flat, doing God knows what. When I came back in the evening, you looked wide-eyed and frantic, like you hadn't left the house all day. You said you dreamed of Rio, every single night, but the Rio in your dreams wasn't real: the trees were too green and the sea was too blue, and its beauty overwhelmed you. And then the angels came back, you said, and your mother's broken tin roof. They seemed to be saying something to you, but you couldn't work it out.

Your English improved and you started to venture out. You found a supermarket that sold black beans and farofa, so you made feijoada, according to your mother's recipe. I introduced you to Susanna, my friend Tom's Brazilian girlfriend, at the pub. When she said, '*Ola Carolina, tudo bom?*' you exhaled deeply, like you'd been holding your breath for three months. You talked to each other all night.

Autumn came, and Susanna helped you to find a job at a fancy hotel, as a chambermaid; a friend of a friend told her about the vacancy, and you were ushered in, no questions asked. Your English was good enough, by then, to answer basic questions, but you told me that mostly you didn't interact with customers, other than smiling at them as they walked past in the corridor. You earned more money than you or your mother had ever earned before, combined, and you made friends with your colleagues: maids, cooks, and porters.

You started going out with them, to parties you grudgingly invited me to, where I would be the only English person there. You didn't see Susanna as much.

'She's a rich girl,' you said.

'Does it matter?' I said.

'Of course it does.'

London was getting darker, greyer; those few days of blueness became fewer and farther between. The temperature hovered below zero and the streets were caked in ice. I bought you a warm, long coat for Christmas, and you smiled your real smile. One night you said to me that you couldn't understand why people flocked from all over the world to live, huddled in coats, herded like livestock on the tube.

'Well, you came,' I said.

'I came for you.'

'Are you going to stay for me?'

You pursed your lips.

We sat there, not speaking, for a while, until you said, in English, 'I dreamed of the angels again.'

'Oh yeah? What did they do?'

And you told me, but you had to slip back into Portuguese, that this time, they had burst through the white ceiling of our bedroom in Brockley. The plaster and wood crashed into pieces and fell at our sides, never hitting us — apparently, I stayed asleep throughout — and you saw the black sky, which was so clear for London, dotted with millions of stars. One of these stars seemed to be growing, expanding its white light, until it flashed and there appeared the angels, all four of them, hovering against the sky.

'Come back, Carolina,' they whispered. 'Come back.'

106

The morning after you told me about the dream, the sky was white and rain speckled the windows. I slept in late, woke up alone and then found you in the living room, watching children's TV and eating jam on toast, drinking Earl Grey, like a British girl. You looked up, and I could see that you had been crying, and your face was paler than it had ever been. Our eyes met and I knew it was over.

'*Bom dia*,' you said, and sipped your tea.

'So what happens now?' I said.

'I'm going home.'

'I'll buy you the ticket.'

'I can buy it myself,' you said, and a tear fell down your cheek. 'I thought you might try to change my mind.'

I slept on the sofa for a week, and then you were gone. I didn't even drive you to the airport: just put you in a cab, kissed you on the cheek and handed over some cash, and only when the car disappeared down the road did I realise my mistake. I emailed to apologise, but you didn't write back.

That was some time ago. I ended up becoming all the things I thought I wouldn't be when I spotted you on Ipanema beach: a husband, a father, a man in a suit on the tube at eight AM. I wonder whether you married, whether you found a better job, or whether you're still up in the hills, sleeping next to your sister under that tin roof. I wonder whether you still dream of angels and I wonder what they say to you.

Here's a short, punchy story from Fiction Desk newcomer William Thirsk-Gaskill. The lesson that Mr Woolley is trying to give in the story actually sounds rather interesting.

Can We Have You All Sitting Down, Please?

William Thirsk-Gaskill

My name is Mason Bentley. I'm a student at Stainbeck College of Tertiary Education. I do maths, geology, and information and communication technology. ICT is my favourite lesson. The teacher is called Mr Woolley.

I am at my desk, and I can see Mr Woolley now, peering through the safety glass panel in the door of the classroom. The students have all arrived – those that can be bothered to turn up. Mr Woolley arrives last, and his face is red and a bit sweaty, as usual.

Mr Woolley can be funny, sometimes. This is the first funny thing about him: how long it takes him to get into the classroom. He looks as if he is counting how many people he can see inside. I don't mean counting like teachers count when they want to know how many sheets or how many books to hand out. It is more like the way I would look at a group of teenagers hanging around the entrance to a subway. Then he just stands there for a moment, holding his briefcase and the files he keeps the lesson in. I don't know what he is doing while he stands there. He puts his briefcase down, turns the door handle with his free hand, and pushes the briefcase through the door in front of him with this foot. Most of the students don't notice him: they just carry on with whatever they are doing.

He puts his stuff down on the teacher's desk, and says, 'Can we have you all sitting down, please?' He says it in his normal voice, which is not very loud. The only person who hears him is me. I line my notepad up with the edge of the desk, and I put my pen next to the pad, and I look at Mr Woolley to let him know that I'm listening to him, but he is not looking at me. He is looking at Jade Kennington, Gilbert Owusu, and Aaron Braithwaite. They are standing up, or sitting astride their chairs, with their backs to him, arguing over something on someone's smartphone; I think it is an app that one of them has downloaded. 'Can we have you all sitting down, please?' He says it again, a bit louder.

'Listen to this cool app,' says Jade. She presses a button on her smartphone. The speaker makes some noise that I don't believe anybody could recognise or understand: it just sounds like a random crackle.

'What is it?' asks Gilbert.

'It's an app that says "Shut up!" in fifty different languages.'

'What was that one?' asks Gilbert Owusu.

'Ukra. Ukree-ann-ian. Something foreign,' say Jade. Gilbert guffaws.

'Give it here,' he says, and tries to grab the phone from Jade's hand.

'Can we have you all sitting down, please? Can we have you all sitting down, please?' Mr Woolley says it still a bit louder.

'What's the point of telling someone to shut up in a language they can't understand?' says Gilbert.

'Oh, never mind. It's just a cool app, that's all.'

'Can we have you all sitting down and facing the front, please?' Now they go and sit down, slowly. It is difficult to tell if they sit down because of what Mr Woolley said, or if they just decided they were going to do it anyway.

Mr Woolley goes quiet for a bit, and puts his files, and his ring-binders, and the wooden box he keeps his pens in, on the desk. People start whispering and talking again. Jade Kennington has started another conversation. As she talks, she brushes her hair and looks at herself in a mirror she has placed on the desk in front of her.

Usually, Mr Woolley has a file in front of him in the middle of the desk with the day's lesson in it. Last week we did 'packet switching', which I think we should be doing again today, because it is quite an important topic. Today, he has two files: one on the left and one on the right. He looks from one to the other. He holds his hand over the files. He wiggles his hand from side to side, as if he has just burnt his finger, but it is a long time before he picks one up. He picks up the file on the right. He moves the file to the centre of the desk, opens it, and then goes to the whiteboard and starts drawing a diagram about packet switching. I write the date at the top of a new page, and start copying the diagram onto my notepad. Mr Woolley explains the diagram, but I can't hear all of what he is saying because Jade Kennington is having an argument with the person sitting behind her.

Mr Woolley has stopped talking and is looking at us, at the class. I look at his eyes, which appear big behind the lenses of his glasses, and I try to work out who he is looking at. He looks at Jade. He looks at Aaron Braithwaite, and then he looks back to Jade. Both Jade and Aaron are concentrating on their smartphones. Mr Woolley puts down his marker pen and watches them.

He stands in front of the whiteboard, quite still. He doesn't usually do this. He either sits behind the teacher's desk, or he moves between the desk and the whiteboard, bouncing from one to the other like one of those little wind-up bumper cars I used to have when I was a kid.

I think I have worked out what Mr Woolley is watching. Jade presses a button on her smartphone, and smirks to herself, and then you can faintly hear the buzz of Aaron's phone vibrating to show that he's received a text message. He reads it, and laughs, and then he presses some buttons on his phone, and so on. Mr Woolley walks between the desks. It looks at first as if he is going to the back of the room to do something with the window. I have never noticed before, but the soles of Mr Woolley's shoes don't make any noise when he walks. A few of the students look curiously at Mr Woolley. They look at him like he is an old, blind Labrador with no collar that had wondered into the college. Jade and Aaron don't notice him at all: they just carry on sending texts to each other.

Mr Woolley grabs the phone out of Jade Kennington's hand. She is taller and probably stronger than Mr Woolley, but he takes her by surprise. He glances at the screen, and his face goes red. His mouth turns down at the corners. He turns his back on the class, and struggles with something. He is doing something with Jade's phone. He pulls the phone's battery out. It slips from his grasp and slides across the floor. He gives the dead phone back to Jade, walks over and picks up the battery, and puts it in his trouser pocket.

'You may collect your battery when the lesson is over,' he says. His voice sounds strange, like he's got a really bad sore throat. Jade is speechless. She looks stunned for a minute, and then she starts laughing. She looks at each of her friends in turn, shrugs, and laughs.

Mr Woolley goes back to the front of the classroom. He rubs the diagram off the whiteboard. He puts all the sheets that he has taken out of the file back in it. He closes the file, turns round, and drops the file in the litter bin. He moves the other file to the centre of the desk, and opens it.

'Alan Mathison Turing was born in London in 1912. He graduated with a degree in mathematics from King's College, Cambridge, in 1934,' says Mr Woolley. Nobody in the class is listening to him, except me. I start writing down the key points in what Mr Woolley is saying: dates, names, important words. 'Turing is regarded as the father of modern computing.' I write that down as well. I can't remember the last time Mr Woolley said the word 'father'.

Among the class, there are no fights or arguments going on, and nobody is playing music or a loud video game, but they are talking among themselves as if Mr Woolley is not here. For the first time that I can remember, he doesn't seem to mind. He carries on talking in a voice that I can only just hear above the background noise. He talks to the back of the room. He talks to the side of the room. He notices me, and he talks to me. He writes a few points on the whiteboard. When he is not writing on the whiteboard, instead of bouncing back and forth between the whiteboard and the teacher's desk, he walks round to the front of the desk and leans against it, facing me, which is good because it means he is a bit nearer and I can hear more of what he is saying.

'Turing was a fascinating figure. Something of a mysterious figure,' says Mr Woolley. I don't write this down, because it isn't really a fact and I know it already. I know a bit about Alan Turing. I am waiting for Mr Woolley to stop talking for a moment, so I can ask him a question. He talks for a long time about World War Two, and the German Enigma machine, which the Nazis thought could encrypt a message in a way that was unbreakable. He talks about how the codebreakers at Bletchley Park could break the code just by working on paper with their brains, but they needed to do it faster and more efficiently, and so they developed machines to do it. And that is how computers started. 'That's why we are here, in this lesson,' says Mr Woolley. He pauses, and looks round the room. Aaron Braithwaite has put his headphones on and is playing a video game. Jade Kennington, without her smartphone, is sitting and staring into space. Gilbert Owusu is pretending to play drums as he listens to his MP3 player. I want Mr Woolley to get through the parts to do with the war so that I can ask him how Alan Turing died. But Mr Woolley is hardly saying anything. He keeps pausing, and looking round the room. 'What do you think they were fighting for? All those soldiers, sailors, airmen. All those merchant seamen, fighter pilots, bomber crews, tank crews, artillery men. All those factory workers, ARP wardens, home guard, medics, nurses. What do you think they were fighting for?' I can't tell whether he is talking to me or not, even though I am the only person who is listening. 'And why do you think they developed electronic machines, capable of being configured to perform a range of tasks by means of the stored instructions that we now refer to as software?

'I'll tell you why. It was so that Aaron Braithwaite could sit through the entire lesson with his headphones on, playing *Call of Duty* — something profoundly ironic about that title, here, I can't help thinking. It was so that he and Jade Kennington could sit and play text tennis, and speculate in the most prurient and offensive manner on whether the tutor is what they are pleased to refer to as a "cheese-gobbler". Given that they find the practice of homosexuality so fascinating, it is a pity they cannot be bothered to listen to what I am saying, because Alan Turing was, in fact, a homosexual.' A few of the class stop talking for a moment, glance nervously at Mr Woolley, and then carry on talking. 'He was prosecuted for being a homosexual in 1952. It is believed that MI5 considered him to be a security risk, because of his susceptibility to blackmail. He died in 1954, of cyanide poisoning. We cannot be certain what caused this – '

'Sir?' says Jade Kennington.

'Yes, Jade.'

'Why are you telling us this?'

'Because it's interesting.'

'It isn't interesting at all, sir. You're just spouting off about some dork we've never heard of.'

'Jade, I am very sorry you feel that way. I am sure somebody in the class finds it interesting. Does anybody find the subject of Alan Turing's contribution to electronic computing, or his mysterious death, interesting?'

'I do, sir,' I say.

'Thank you, Mason. I was sure I could rely on you.' Somebody says something which I don't quite catch. It might have been, 'He can rely on Mason Bentley to suck him off.' Mr Woolley just carries on talking. 'Whether you regard Alan Turing's career as an interesting subject or not, you cannot deny the impact that his pioneering work has had on our lives. Every time you go on YouTube to watch skateboarding cats, every time you download pornography, or pirated music or videos, every time you go online to buy anything, book anything, check a timetable, or place an underage bet, you are using technology which derives from Turing's work.' It is coming up to the end of the lesson. The other students get ready to leave the classroom, which makes even more noise than when they are talking. They don't wait for Mr Woolley to tell them they can go. They just put their coats on, pick up their bags and leave with a scraping of chair legs. Jade Kennington goes up to Mr Woolley and asks for her phone battery. He hands it to her. As the class crowds round the door, waiting to get out, I am the only one still sitting and listening. 'And, had it not been for the intelligence obtained from the breaking of the Enigma cipher, this country would now be ruled by Nazis, and we would have no freedom to do any of these things. Every aspect of life, certainly including mobile communication, would be under constant surveillance and control by the state.'

I want him to look at me and carry on talking, but he doesn't. Once the crowd of students has left and the door is clear, Mr Woolley picks up his stuff and leaves. There is no other class waiting to come in, and so I just sit there with my pad and pen on the desk in front of me. I sit there for a long time.

We receive surprisingly few comic stories at The Fiction Desk, and even fewer that are any good. They're hard to write and possibly even harder to find a home for. Once in a while we do manage to get our hands on a gem though, like 'Rex' in Various Authors, or Mike Scott Thomson's story below.

Me, Robot

Mike Scott Thomson

I feel ridiculous. I look like a pillock, sitting right here with you boys.

Yeah, I know, that's the least of my worries right now. I'm in the shit. I get it.

Ever had a robot here before? I bet you've had all sorts. No? Not surprised, mate.

Okay, let's get on with it. From the start, then.

I guess you've already checked my records and know about my previous. I should come clean about that, first up.

Yeah that's right pal, it was only the beginning of this month. Bakerloo Line. I'd taken the Sunday afternoon shift — quiet, no bother, a chance to get away from the grief I was getting at home — and had driven my train from Elephant & Castle to Lambeth North. Sure, I should have been concentrating. I should have known the doors failed to open at Lambeth North, but hardly no one ever gets on and off there, right? 'Specially not on a Sunday afternoon. So at Waterloo, when I do remember to open the doors, some posh herbert in a tweed jacket and a gold tooth in his gob comes waddling up to the cab, raps on the window and calls me a lazy, incompetent, good-for-nothing waste of skin.

All because he went one stop too far? Please. Such disrespect. That's what gets me: a lack of basic manners, ya know what I mean? And with everything going to shit with Sandra back home, the red mist descended. So I leap out of the cab and give him a right hook, thwack, smack on the kisser. Down he went like a rag doll onto the platform, and I climbed back in and carried on towards Embankment.

Anyway, he pressed charges, and yeah, I got the sack. After fifteen years. Charming. Never in trouble with the law before that. You boys know that, right?

But here's the thing. Sandra still don't know. About getting the sack, that is. She thought I just had my knuckles rapped. So I went in the next day, got fired, but stayed out drinking coffee in that depressing shopping centre in Elephant until it was the end of, supposedly, my shift. Went home like it was a normal day. Slept in on the Tuesday, left the house at noon for my afternoon, well, shift. Loitered around the mall again, drank crap coffee.

I couldn't tell her. Just... couldn't, mate. Not after everything we'd been through the past year. I really tried, I did man, I promise.

Okay, so I made a mistake with the paint. Scarlet was for the hallway, sky blue for the bedroom. I know that now. 'It's like sleeping in a bloody slaughterhouse,' she kept whining.

Then what? Oh yeah, the cheese and wine party with her book club. Yeah, it would have been better if I'd remembered to buy the cheese. Come on, allow me that, man.

And that god-awful weekend break we had in Moorgate. How was I to know she wanted to visit Margate? 'Did the beach towels

I packed not even give you the tiniest hint?' she yammered, over and over again.

She accuses me of not listening, of not thinking, of not having a heart. Dude, that hurts. How can anyone react to that?

So me getting fired — me, the breadwinner — I couldn't say nothing, you understand? So, I signed on. No shame in that: I paid my taxes before. May as well get some of them back now. Rainy day, right? But I needed more; something to top up my dole money so she wouldn't notice. Until I found something better.

Then I remembered. Back when things were still good between Sandra and me, we'd had that day out on the London Eye and a stroll along the South Bank, and there were loads of these performers: breakdancers, magicians, jugglers, you know the sort, right? And they were raking it in. All these people crowding around, clapping, laughing, taking photos... and giving away their money. Well, it's showbusiness, innit?

Now I can't do any of those things — juggle and what-have-you — but there's one thing I can do very well, as a result of doing pretty much the same thing in the driver's cab over hundreds of Tube journeys down the years, and that is, well, stay really bloody still. That afternoon by the Thames, there was one guy, he'd sprayed himself head-to-toe in gold paint and was just stood there. Motionless, mainly. Occasionally he'd move, his limbs stiff like a robot, and summat or another would buzz at the same time, a whirr. Bzzz! Bzzz! And Sandra and me, we laughed like a drain, and had our photo taken with him.

It's probably the last photo of us both looking happy.

Anyway, I looked at this guy then, saw how much money was in his pot and thought to myself, how hard can it be?

So the next week, the week after I got the sack, I went shopping. Went to a party shop, got some tins of silver body paint. Went to some charity shops, got some old clothes no one wanted no more, they didn't have to look cool 'cos I was going to spray them anyway, right? Found a top hat, some old silver sunglasses, gloves, a Tupperware pot for the tips. An old pair of boots. A banana crate from the market to stand on. Called my mate Davey Boy, the sculptor, he did that wadjuma-call-it outside Ikea, ya know? He let me borrow his studio, told me I could deck myself out there whenever I needed to and shower myself off afterwards.

I'm sure he was suppressing a chuckle that first time. Cheeky sod. Anyway, who cares, I thought. I was earning a living again.

And ya know what? I'm really good at it. That first day I went to Croydon town centre, the pedestrianised bit outside the shopping arcade. Bright and early on the Friday — yeah, only yesterday, in fact. Went to Davey Boy's, got myself dressed in my silver gear, spray painted my face, put my top hat on, took my crate, I was away. Yeah, I looked a pillock riding the tram from Addington Village, but I didn't give a monkeys. I have a thick skin, ya know? And with a load of silver paint, it was now even thicker. I set the crate down on the paving stones, stepped on and stayed really bloody still.

I made fifty quid that day. Fifty smackers, my son! You wouldn't have thought it, would ya? But the cash kept coming. The folks in Croydon, they have a bad rep, but they loved it. Good as gold, they were. They laughed when I suddenly made stiff movements, like the gold robot I'd seen way back when, buzzing through my lips. Bzzz! Bzzz! Nothing to it. Kiddies and old grannies had a smile on their face as they passed by. Geezers wanted their photo taken. Punk kids heckled a bit, sure they did — I was called a wanker more than once — but I didn't deck them. Those kids, they ain't never worth it.

That's not to say everything went swell. It was hot and the paint made me even hotter; I made a mental note not to wear so many layers. I also remembered to keep my wallet in my back rather than front pocket — more than once some punk kid tried to pick me until I bzzz'd myself to the side — and I realised quite soon I had to keep the tip bowl a few feet away, since most folks, the decent ones, they don't like to get too close. But otherwise pukka, mate. I was in a new game.

I got home that evening, after showering and changing at Davey's mind, and Sandra was none the wiser. So I thought, I'll do some more of this. Let's go for the big one!

I told her, I gotta do a Saturday shift, old Pete's poorly again so I said I'd cover. And so this very morning, I silvered myself up at Davey's, took the train to Elephant — me, this silver dude amongst all the weekend shoppers — and got on the Tube, the same train I'd once driven, up to Waterloo. By nine o'clock I was a few yards away from the London Eye, and I admit it, although I'm a geezer, a small tear did come to my eye as I remembered that happy day I'd spent with my darling on that wheel all those months ago. But I brushed it away, otherwise the silver paint would've run down my cheek see, and stood on my crate opposite Jubilee Gardens.

Man, it was way busier than Croydon. I was going to make a mint. There were tourists... hundreds of them. French, Spanish, Japanese, Americans, all filing past, crowding round, smiling, taking photos — and giving me their cash. Every so often I bzzz'd my arms and twisted my body round, and the folks would laugh and throw money in the pot. I was competing for their attentions with the body poppers a bit further down, and the old magic man with the cups and balls, and the fire eater on the unicycle, but I was holding my own. One hour gone and I must've made twenty big ones already.

Then I saw her. Or rather, I saw them.

Sandra. And some dude, the same one I'd decked in Lambeth North. That tall, chubby herbert in a tweed jacket. I knew it was him 'cos he was grinning like the Cheshire Cat and I could see his gold tooth, and he had his arm round her, coming out of the crowd by the London Eye. Chance had it, at that moment I was turned in their direction, both my arms pointing robot-like towards the wheel, and my line of vision was level with them.

And no, I couldn't do nothing. If anything I stayed stiller than I had been previously, but my heart, the heart that Sandra was saying I didn't have, I felt it, man, I felt it burst into a million little bits. No, I thought to myself, me, the silver man, the robot, not my Sandra. Not her. Not him.

And what made it worse? They got to me, my eyes turned as far back as possible in my head to watch them, and they laughed. Both of them. 'Wow!' said Sandra to this fella who was now touching her arse, 'A silver man! C'mon! Let's get a photo!' And they grabbed this Japanese tourist, and there they stood, either side of me, and I had to bzzz round to face the camera, my arms sticking up either side. And the Japanese guy took the photo with the camera I'd bought for her birthday and grinned and bowed, and my darling bowed to him by way of thanks, and her and the posh herbert turned back to me, chuckled again, gave me a wave and off they went, arm in fucking arm, and didn't even tip me neither.

I stood there for a while longer, my brain cloudy, sick to my stomach. I couldn't think; I couldn't even act like a robot no more. I just stood there, a statue, two tiny tears in both eyes, hidden behind my sunglasses, and I couldn't even wipe them.

So it was a bad time for the gold robot to make an appearance and give it the big I-am.

'Oi!' he said, appearing out of nowhere. 'That's my spot! Who are you?!'

Now, my heart may have been smashed to pieces, but I stayed in character, see; that was already force of habit. I bzzz'd my left arm up — bzzz — and shook my head — bzzz, bzzz, bzzz. My middle finger extended from my silver fist. Bzzz. Up yours, golden boy.

He didn't like that much. 'Wise guy, eh?' he snapped, this gold fella having beef with a silver one. We must've looked quite a picture. 'Well then,' he carried on, 'tell me this, sunshine. Where's your busker's licence?' And then, just to rub salt into the wound, 'And ya call that a robot? That's a good-for-nothing waste of paint.'

Busker's licence? I had no idea, honest. But that small matter barely crossed my mind as I buzzed my right arm up and back — bzzz, bzzz — clenched my fist — bzzz — and gave him a right hook — BZZZ! — smack in the kisser. He fell to the floor, clump, his top hat sent flying, and it was just as he clambered back to his feet and about to clout me one back that you boys arrived and dragged me away.

So there ya have it.

Oh, you're granting me bail? Who's putting it up?

Oh no, please. Not her. Not now. Not like this.

Please, Sarge.

Please.

*Matt Plass contributed the title story to our previous
anthology,* The Maginot Line, *and walked off with the
Fiction Desk Writer's Award for his trouble. You can imagine
how pleased I was to get my hands on this new story.*

Tripe Soup and Spanish Wine

Matt Plass

The guest list reads like an unexploded bomb. But I shouldn't
even be looking: it's Edgar's computer and we don't do that. So I
gather the coffee mugs, the small plates with toast crumbs, and I
back out of the study.

Over dinner, I ask Edgar if he's thought much about next
Friday.

'Still conflicted about the main,' he says.

I ask how many people. Edgar scrapes the sauce jug with his
knife and draws the blunt edge along his tongue. 'Too much
fennel,' he says. 'Six. So we don't have to borrow chairs.'

I start to clear. Edgar watches, his long face heavy in the
lamplight. I ask if he's winning.

'You tell me. Or we could ask the quack.'

The Wednesday before the dinner party and Edgar has been
shopping. There are two empty Sainsbury's bags in the cupboard

under the stairs, two paper packages in the fridge. No labels. He's been to the Turkish shop; unfamiliar spices crowd the middle shelf. I ask what's on the menu. He tells me wait and see, his face more animated than I've seen in a while. I tell myself that Friday is a good idea.

Thursday evening in the kitchen. Edgar has opened two bottles of red. An empty water carafe stands between them.

'Châteaux Prieure Lichine.' He decants one bottle into the carafe. 'Forty-two pounds a pop.'

Edgar's nose wrinkles as he lifts the second bottle with finger and thumb. 'And this, the wine that dare not speak its name. *Spanish Table Wine*. From, ah, *one of Europe's premier vineyards*. A promise of *rich fruity notes* and change from three quid.'

Edgar places the Spanish mouth to the French and eases the cheap wine into the expensive bottle. He reads my face, grins and pulls his fingers into pretend dinosaur claws, 'Don't be such an Anxiousaurus, Maggie. It's a Pepsi Challenge. By the way, kitchen's off limits tomorrow.'

Friday evening. Our guests fill the lounge and I've done my best to feign surprise. Edgar is effervescent; the old Edgar who fusses over scarves and coats and insists on making the perfect gin and tonic. I'm allowed back in the kitchen to fetch beer from the fridge. Under copper lids, two pots rattle on the hob. I lift a lid, release a cloud of umber gas. It's sharp, agricultural. From the other room, I hear Jeannette scold Hobbs for spilling gin.

We take our places in the dining room: Joel and Kay, Hobbs and Jeannette, Neil and his new girlfriend, Rashmi. At the head of the table, Edgar taps his glass with a knife.

'Objection, Your Honour,' says Hobbs, flicking a nail against his own empty tumbler. 'Speeches verboten.'

Edgar tips an imaginary hat. 'Consider it your entrance fee.'

Joel asks what happened to the man of few words.

'And the master of none,' adds Joel's wife, Kay.

Yes, it's forced banter, but you have to turn the handle sometimes. I realise I've been holding my breath and ration it out through tight lips.

'Comrades,' says Edgar. 'We have a new gorilla in our midst so allow me. This is Rashmi. Rashmi, the heavy gent to my left is Joel, fallen solicitor turned house-spouse cum child-wrangler.' Joel winces at *fallen*, but judges it to have passed unnoticed. He salutes with his glass.

Edgar swings right to introduce, 'Kay, Joel's ambrosial wife, a thespian.' He pronounces thespian to rhyme with lesbian. 'For years a dim footlight, but now, oh em gee, Kay has dipped a painted toe into the mire of television.'

Kay sticks out her tongue. Rashmi, small featured with hair pinned tight behind her ears, studies Kay, trying to place her.

'House Alert,' says Joel. 'On Sky Living.'

Rashmi cracks an *ah, yes* smile.

Kay says, 'Rashmi is now displaying what we call the House Alert Face: the one you pull as you recall clicking past House Alert on your way to a programme you like on a channel you watch. Pity, I left the BAFTA in the car.'

'It keeps the lights on,' says Joel.

'Faint praise indeed,' says Edgar. Joel and Kay share a spousal look. Joel breaks off first.

Edgar turns to Neil, so tall he stoops even when sitting down. 'We haven't seen Neil in a while. Tell me, Rashmi, behind the lank, dirty hair does there still lurk a lank and dirty mind? And that dreadful fish tattoo?'

Neil pulls back his hair to reveal his neck and, yes, the tattoo is poor. '*Je ne regrette* nothing,' he says.

'Is Neil still in sustainable development?' Edgar twists the last two words. 'And does he still smoke cigarettes?'

'I am here,' says Neil.

'Yes to the first,' says Rashmi. 'Sadly, yes to the second,'

'Never mind. Now, as the new girl, aside from the discovery that you are prepared to be seen in public with Neil, we know little of you. Yet. Rashmi, you have been warned. Shall we eat?'

Hobbs coughs twice and raps the table with his knuckle.

Edgar mugs an apology but something dark flits across his eyes. 'Forgive me,' he says. 'To Maggie's left we have Hobbs who is a crumbling alcoholic. Opposite Hobbs, his carping wife, Jeanette, who drove him there.'

Rashmi starts to smile: a joke, surely? But even for these first time acquaintances Edgar's words ring so true. And the rest of us, our frozen faces, six sharp intakes of breath: we drive the nail home.

'I've known Hobbs since Durham. He's in bathrooms.'

Jeanette turns to me for sanction but Hobbs draws himself up to retaliate. 'Planning to drain the State for long, Edgar? Or are you feeling better?'

'Oh, muchly.' Edgar is already half way through the door to the kitchen.

In the time it takes Edgar to bring the starter I say, 'Bear with him. This is progress.' Six nods from around the table.

I dip into Hobbs' line of sight. 'It's because he feels safest with you.'

Hobbs frowns and pours a second glass of white but leaves it on the cloth. The kitchen door swings open and Edgar is here with the two-handled tureen. He heaves it (with a liquid slosh, like a fat man getting out of a bath) onto the centre of the table and lifts the lid, releasing that sweet-but-animal odour.

'Smells complicated,' says Joel.

Edgar wields the ladle. He initiates a carousel, sending full bowls around the table. Mine arrives filled with muddy liquor. A lump of coral-combed flesh slips beneath the surface. I prod it with my spoon, half expecting it to swim away.

Seven people stare at their soup. The eighth says, 'Dig in.'

I load my spoon, feel my abdomen knot. With the metal at my lips the aroma is... (I'm nine, a tennis holiday, probably Bournemouth. Between my toes a virile fungus spreads, till now hidden from my parents. The doctor has very black eyes. He tells my mother it's usually only retarded children who struggle with basic hygiene.)

Edgar's watches me. They all do. I swallow, take it down and keep it there. I even manage a smile.

'Iskembe,' says Edgar. 'Turkish delicacy.'

'Only a Turk could eat it,' says Hobbs to Neil.

Neil reminds Hobbs that he, Neil, loves Turkish food, and culture, and people. Hobbs grunts, points at Neil's soup and tells him he's in luck then. That's all the sparring they can manage.

Edgar studies the six pristine liquid surfaces. 'As you know,' he says, 'I have of late lost all my mirth. But to be sat here again with friends...' His chin drops to his chest, the head shakes. '... It isn't unappreciated.'

Hobbs makes a sound between a cough and a curse. Jeannette places a hand over her husband's and gives it a squeeze, smiles at Edgar and takes up her spoon. We all do the same except Joel who dips a piece of bread. Kay glares at Joel: *no cheating.*

We spoon, sip, swallow in silence. As Kay says later, how could we talk? We were too focused on overriding our digestive systems. When every bowl has a respectable tidemark, the spoons go down. My mouth is a cow shed.

Kay stiffens at the sight of Edgar's bowl. 'You haven't touched yours.'

Edgar tours his guests with solemn eyes. Then he says, 'It's tripe. *Bleuch*. I can't eat tripe.'

We time-out between courses. Edgar disappears upstairs. Neil heads for the garden patting his pockets. Rashmi helps me clear the starter while Joel investigates and comments (to no one) on Edgar's vinyl. Kay and Jeanette remain at the table. Jeanette has a hundred questions for Kay about television. They all begin with *have you met...?* Within thirty seconds, Hobbs needs fresh air.

When we reassemble, Edgar has an uncorked bottle. His hand obscures the label. 'Blind taste challenge, Hobbs?' He walks behind Joel and Rashmi. 'I've been saving this.'

Edgar pours half a glass for Hobbs who wraps his fist around the stem and announces himself ready.

As Hobbs lifts his glass to the light, Rashmi says she came *this* close to buying a book on wine last year.

'Looks like it comes from the left side of the vineyard, but south of the water trough,' Hobbs tells Rashmi. Then, fast, before she can make a fool of herself, he says, 'Joke! Although, on the big three: nation, region, and grape, my batting average is respectable.'

'We do the *Times* tasting days,' says Jeannette.

Hobbs does know wine; I suppose it's his cover story. From the moment he lifts the glass his brow pinches. He swirls, sniffs, sips, purses his lips, swills it back to bathe his wisdom teeth, pulls a sour face. Hobbs winks at me and swallows.

'Repugnant. Supermarket slurry. You got me with that rancid soup, Ed, but fool me twice shame on me. Let's have the kosher bottle.'

The corners of Edgar's lips turn down as he spins the label to face us. 'This is second mortgage vino. Supposed to be a great year.'

Hobbs reaches for the bottle, sniffs the neck. 'Corked.'

'No,' says Edgar.

'That is not Châteaux Prieure Lichine,' says Hobbs. But the bottle is there on the table.

'To err is human,' says Edgar. He snatches up the bottle, takes three long steps to the sideboard and produces a bottle of Marks & Spencer's red, then announces a ten minute wait on the main. Hobbs studies his nails while Edgar removes the cork and pours.

The quiet proves unsustainable. Two conversations grind into life. I half listen to Jeannette's frustration with her mobile phone provider, but find myself tuning into the other end of the table where Joel is saying, '... like when you hear a man say he's babysitting his own kids.'

Rashmi agrees, 'As if he's doing his wife a favour.'

'Well he is, isn't he?' says Edgar.

Joel responds to Rashmi. 'Exactly. I do miss the office chat, the whole drinks after work scenario. But the flip side: I see all Sam's firsts and we do cool stuff together. On Tuesday, the little toad got his mitts on... ah!' Joel has expansive hands and his wine glass was too close. He swears and heads to the kitchen for a cloth.

In my right ear Hobbs is asking Kay about theatre versus television.

'Theatre is more of this.' Kay turns up the corners of her mouth with two fingers. 'TV is more of that.' She rubs her thumb and forefinger together. Jeannette and I share a smile as we watch Hobbs screw down the urge to ask Kay what she earns.

Edgar appears at a crouch between Hobbs and Kay. 'Hobbs, did you know Kay was an ugly sister in Broadstairs?'

'And Ophelia that summer,' I say.

Edgar says that Hobbs does a lot of acting. Hobbs shakes his head, nope.

'It's true. Every morning, when Hobbs arrives at work he acts sober.'

Hobbs places both hands flat on the table cloth.

'Play nice,' Kay says into her glass. I ask Edgar if I can have a word in the kitchen, but he's locked onto Kay. 'Joel was just telling us about the new arrangement.'

No response.

'Must be tough for him, handing over the hunter-gatherer badge.'

'Joel did his time,' says Kay. 'I earned four-fifths of fuck all for years.'

'Imagine, stuck at home with the nipper, watching old Poirots while your wife is out making bacon.'

'He's dealt with it very well, doesn't seem to be an issue. Jeannette, tell me about something.'

Joel is back with a damp cloth, dabbing at his wine spill. Edgar tells him his ears must be burning.

'It's all true,' says Joel. 'Or it's a pack of damn lies.'

'We were discussing trad roles *dans la maison*. How hard it must be for you, stuck at home with little Sam while Kay builds a career in the media. Kay says... don't you Kay... Kay says you're dealing with it very well.'

Kay rubs her eyes. Joel looks at her, hard.

'In context please,' she says. But Edgar has moved on to Neil, asking him what happened to that girl we met last year.

'The one with the hair, from the Eco-ship; we liked her vowel sounds. And what about the girl before her, the fat Demi Moore?'

Neil blows imaginary smoke at the ceiling. Edgar turns to Rashmi, gives her his kindest smile. 'Did Neil meet you online, too?'

Rashmi places a hand on Neil's forearm, tells him it's okay. A buzzer sounds in the kitchen. Edgar says, 'Time for the main act.' He leaves us frozen but soon returns carrying a silver salver with a high domed lid. We don't own a silver salver. He's bought a silver salver just for tonight. I refill my glass, spill a little and watch it spread like blood.

The salver sits in the centre of the table, candlelight dancing on the dome. Edgar doesn't remove the lid. If this is a movie, the next thing we see is a ghosted human face with a bloody rim where the neck should be. The room suffers a momentary surge in gravity.

Edgar lifts the dome. Beneath the lid is a nest of four boiled deer's heads, eyeballs seared in place, skin stippled, the grey meat flaking, steam piping from the nostrils as if the animals are breathing hard in the cold, near the end of the chase.

'Continuing the international theme,' says Edgar, 'This is Icelandic. I can't spell it, neither can I pronounce it. But I can show you how to eat it. One between two, by the way.'

He forks soft flesh, just above the eyes. A turn of the wrist shreds meat from bone and pulls upwards on the eye sockets. The poor, dead creature watches the flaying of its own skull.

As Edgar lifts his prize, Rashmi pushes back from the table. Someone, probably Neil, buries a retch.

Hobbs snaps. 'Enough.' He tips back his chair and disappears through the kitchen and into the garden.

Kay says, 'I won't eat it.' To me she mouths, 'Sorry.'

Jeannette has placed her knife and fork on her plate at twenty past four. I turn to Joel and fix him with shameless, begging eyes. Joel, proud carnivore, picks up his fork and nods, he can do this. But when he prods at the deer's cheek a chunk of meat slides from the bone to reveal a demonic jaw line; a set of bleached, square teeth. Joel drops the fork.

'Not with it laughing at me.'

Edgar straightens his spine, wraps his hands together and bows his head as if to say grace.

'We got there in the end,' he says.

Hobbs is back in the room, but stays on his feet behind his chair.

'It appears,' says Edgar, 'that my sad little charity dinner is over.' He waves towards the door. 'Sleep well. Duty done.'

Edgar pushes his chair in, mirroring Hobbs' stance with both hands on the seat back. Hobbs sits.

'Don't be a brat, Edgar,' says Kay.

Edgar addresses the ceiling rose. 'Was it too much to hope for? Would it have been too much of an effort to humour me?' He asks if we have any idea how difficult tonight has been for him.

'Not been a pleasure cruise for us,' says Joel.

'My first... What did that little white-coat call it? My first attempt at socialising in a safe environment. You must have been thinking, poor Edgar, but we know what will build his confidence! We'll let him spend days preparing a special, no an *international* meal. Then we'll prod our food round our plates like children at the adults' table.'

'They all came,' I say, something burning the back of my throat. 'They're *here*.'

'Of course they are. What, turn down an opportunity to feel this smug? Neil wouldn't have missed it for all the tobacco in Trinidad, would you, Neil? With your litany of dismal liaisons and your confused, sixth-form politics you don't often get to look down on others. Perhaps that explains Rashmi.

'And less of your disappointed face, Kay. I remember you before you opened supermarkets. Like when you lost that part in Murder Mile and bawled for a week, mostly on our sofa.

'Then there's Joel, caught with a crooked sixpence in his pocket; disbarred, sword snapped over his head and now he's Mr Stay-Home Dad. You, Joel, should know how it feels to fall.'

White flecks mottle the corners of Edgar's mouth. 'Last, worst, is Jeannette,' he says. 'The shrew. And on the other end of her chain is Hobbs, my best friend. Anybody's best friend. That's the problem with a drunk. Hobbs, really, these days what's the point of you?'

I'm on my feet yelling through saltwater, but I don't exist.

Edgar screams. 'All of you. Out.'

He pulls down hard on the back of his chair, slams it to the ground. Plates jump and cutlery falls; a wine glass shatters on the floor. Edgar grips the table edge with both hands, arches his back, buries his head between his biceps and makes a long keening sound; a bull with a sword in its side.

Silence, held breath. For some reason it matters that Edgar and I are the only ones standing. I realise that all evening he hasn't spoken to me, or even looked my way. Whatever happens next has to come from me. But then the doorbell chimes, an alien sound.

Hobbs stands, his face full of decision. 'I'm sorry, Edgar,' he says. 'But I saw where this evening was going. I called someone.' He walks through into the hall. We remain a tableau, Edgar still in his rictus arch.

We hear voices, the front door slams. Hobbs reappears holding two plastic bags and brings with him the scent of cardamom and cumin. He places the bags on his chair and starts to transfer plastic containers onto the table.

'Can someone shift Bambi,' he says. 'I may have over-ordered.'

Joel moves the salver to the sideboard and a mountain of Indian food builds upon the table.

Edgar unwinds his body, stands straight. 'We don't accept foreign aid,' he says in a tight voice.

Hobbs plates up. Joel takes a spoon and helps out. Rashmi does a plate for Edgar, piles it high with korma, rice, spinach. She sets it in front of him. We eat while he stands.

'You may as well tuck in,' says Neil.

'And sit down,' says Kay. 'Making me dizzy.'

Edgar's eyes shine. 'What is this?'

Joel drains his wine, sets down his glass. 'You might remember this, Ed. When Sam was four months he had that brutal chest infection and could hardly breathe, sounded like Darth Vader. Kay and I were in bits. Three or four times a day we had to suck black mucus out through his tiny nose and spit it into the sink.'

'But it was nectar. Because you adored him.'

'It was beyond disgusting.'

'Repulsive,' says Kay.

Edgar shakes his head and tells her, 'No, no, no. Don't you do that. You can't ignore what I said about you all.'

'This isn't about us.'

'Meaning I'm not even worth getting mad at?'

'Meaning you lost, Edgar,' says Hobbs forking a cube of lamb. 'So sit down.'

Edgar sits. He's wary now. And he stays that way: seated, silent, while we work our way through the Indian meal. It takes me, I don't know, lifetimes to process what is happening.

Kay describes her battles with Wardrobe over red stripes. Jeannette tells me about a new girl on the front desk who probably won't last. Joel recalls his disintegration on the day that Sam was born and how, when his particles finally reassembled they did so in new form: a redeemed, adult version of himself.

Neil knows what he means, that sense of upheaval, life shifting gears, new roles. He says he first felt it aged eleven when he found his father crying in the kitchen.

Rashmi talks to Edgar (receiving neither reply nor acknowledgement) about her work, why her car won't pass its next MOT, how best to get across London when the Jubilee line is closed.

All the while Edgar sits and watches. I fetch more wine. The music ends and no one moves. Hobbs makes the deer French-kiss and Kay throws a balled napkin at him. Neil tells a long, funny story about being cut up at traffic lights by a grandmother. I listen, contribute little, floating on their voices; my eyes never leaving Edgar, my husband, as we talk and drink and pick at the food cartons until it's past midnight and the taxis begin to arrive.

About the Contributors

Die Booth lives in Chester and enjoys toy cameras, visiting abandoned places and hunting for the Thing under the bed. After recently co-editing online horror project and anthology 'Re-Vamp' and being published in various anthologies and magazines, Die is currently working on a novel.

Colin Corrigan is a filmmaker and writer living in Dublin. He wrote the short films *Magic* (which he also directed) and *Dead Load*. He has an MA in Creative Writing from UCD, and his first story 'Deep Fat', was published in *The Stinging Fly* magazine.

'Wonders of the Universe' is Colin's second story to appear in a Fiction Desk anthology: 'The Romantic' appeared in *All These Little Worlds*.

Matthew Licht is the author of the detective trilogy *World without Cops*, and several other novels. His short story collection *The Moose Show* (Salt) was nominated for the Frank O'Connor Prize. A new collection, *Justine, Joe & The Zen Garbageman*, is due out soon, again from Salt. He's obsessed with bicycles. Due to this, or as a consequence, he lives in Italy. "Got to burn off the spaghetti somehow."

Matthew's story 'Dave Tough's Luck' appeared in *Various Authors*, the first Fiction Desk anthology.

S R Mastrantone is a writer and musician from Birmingham, now living in Oxford. His stories have been published or are forthcoming in *Stupefying Stories*, *Goldfish Grimm's* and elsewhere. He is currently working on his first novel. When he isn't writing, he can usually be found conducting rock experiments in his band The Woe Betides.

Miha Mazzini is a Slovenian author, with 27 published books, translated in 9 languages. His work was often been anthologised, including in the 2011 Pushcart prize anthology. He's also a screenwriter and director, and voting member of the European Film Academy. He has a PhD in Anthropology of Everyday Life.

Matt Plass lives in Sussex. He works in e-learning, previously edited *Tall Tales & Modern Fables* magazine and is one half of Bread and Love Productions.

Matt is making his second Fiction Desk appearance in this volume: he also wrote the title story in our anthology *The Maginot Line*.

Luiza Sauma was born in Rio de Janeiro and raised in London from the age of four. She recently quit her journalism job to do a Creative and Life Writing MA at Goldsmiths, University of London.

Her short stories have been published in *Litro*, *Untitled Books*, *Notes from the Underground* and others. She's writing a novel set in the Amazon city of Belém. It might take some time.

Richard Smyth is an author and journalist. His stories have appeared in *.cent*, *The Stinging Fly* and *Vintage Script* and are read regularly at the Liars' League in London. Two non-fiction books are in the works: *Bum Fodder*, an illustrated history of toilet paper, will be released by Souvenir Press in November 2012, and *Bloody British History: Leeds* will be published by the History Press in the new year.

As a journalist, he has written features for *New Humanist*, *History Today* and *New Scientist magazines*, among others.

He is represented as a novelist by Peter Buckman at the Ampersand Agency.

Mike Scott Thomson has been a writer for fifteen years. His first published works were commissioned (but highly unauthorised!) biographies of various well-known pop groups — although you'll have to ask him which ones. After this he turned to travel writing, blogging and then fiction. His short stories have so far appeared in *Writers' Forum Magazine*, *Five Stop Story* and *Strange Bounce*.

A resident of Mitcham, Surrey, he works in broadcasting and is a member of three London writers' groups.

William Thirsk-Gaskill needed five attempts before being accepted by The Fiction Desk. He specialises in coming second in short fiction competitions (*Grist 2012* and the *5 Minute Fiction* 1st Birthday competition).

William lives in Wakefield and works as an IT consultant in Leeds. He co-presents a local radio programme in Halifax, called 'Themes for Dreamers'. He has been invited to front the appearance of the *Grist* poets at the 2012 Ted Hughes Festival. He has been commissioned to write a story to be published by Goggle Publishing in 2013.

For more information on the contributors
to this volume, please visit our website:

www.thefictiondesk.com/authors

Also from The Fiction Desk:

Various Authors

the first Fiction Desk anthology

These stories will take you from the shores of Lake Garda in Italy to a hospital room in Utah, from a retirement home overlooking the Solent to an unusual school in the wilds of Scotland. Meet people like Daniel, a government employee looking for an escape; and William, a most remarkable dog by anyone's standards.

Various Authors is the first volume in our new series of anthologies dedicated to discovering and publishing the best new short fiction.

New stories by:

Charles Lambert	Matthew Licht
Lynsey May	Ben Lyle
Jon Wallace	Danny Rhodes
Patrick Whittaker	Harvey Marcus
Adrian Stumpp	Alex Cameron
Jason Atkinson	Ben Cheetham

Avilable to order from all good British bookshops, or online at www.thefictiondesk.com.

£9.99

Out now.

ISBN 9780956784308

Also from The Fiction Desk:

All These Little Worlds

the second Fiction Desk anthology

Among the stories in our second anthology: a new dress code causes havoc in an American school, a newspaper mistake leads a retired comedian to look back over a not-quite-spotless career, and a family buys an unusual addition to their fish tank.

This volume also features 'Pretty Vacant', a special long story from Charles Lambert.

New stories by:

Charles Lambert	Colin Corrigan
Jason Atkinson	Ryan Shoemaker
Halimah Marcus	Jennifer Moore
Andrew Jury	Mischa Hiller
James Benmore	

Avilable to order from all good British bookshops,
or online at www.thefictiondesk.com.

£9.99
Out now.
ISBN 9780956784322

Subscribe

one year - four volumes
for just
£36.95

(wherever you are in the world).

Subscribing to our anthology series is the best way to support
out publishing programme and keep yourself supplied with
the best new short fiction from the UK and abroad. It costs
just £36.95 for a year (four volumes).

We publish a new volume roughly every three months. Each
one has its own title: *Crying Just Like Anybody* is volume four.
The next volume is due early 2013.

Subscribe online:
www.thefictiondesk.com/subscribe

(Price correct at time of going to press, but may change
over time; please see website for current pricing.)